DEATH AND THE OLD MASTER

Also by G.M. Malliet

The St. Just mysteries

DEATH OF A COZY WRITER
DEATH AND THE LIT CHICK
DEATH AT THE ALMA MATER
DEATH IN CORNWALL *
DEATH IN PRINT *

The Max Tudor series

WICKED AUTUMN
A FATAL WINTER
PAGAN SPRING
DEMON SUMMER
THE HAUNTED SEASON
DEVIL'S BREATH
IN PRIOR'S WOOD
THE WASHING AWAY OF WRONGS

The Augusta Hawke mysteries

AUGUSTA HAWKE *
INVITATION TO A KILLER *

Novels

WEYCOMBE

* *available from Severn House*

My Ladybug's Alzheimer's Journey

She Looked Like My Mother, But She Did Not Act Like My Mother

R.D. CARTER

iUniverse, Inc.
Bloomington

My Ladybug's Alzheimer's Journey
She Looked Like My Mother But She Did Not Act
Like My Mother

Copyright © 2010 by R. D. Carter

All rights reserved. No part of this book may be used or reproduced by any means, graphic, electronic, or mechanical, including photocopying, recording, taping or by any information storage retrieval system without the written permission of the publisher except in the case of brief quotations embodied in critical articles and reviews.

iUniverse books may be ordered through booksellers or by contacting:

iUniverse
1663 Liberty Drive
Bloomington, IN 47403
www.iuniverse.com
1-800-Authors (1-800-288-4677)

Because of the dynamic nature of the Internet, any Web addresses or links contained in this book may have changed since publication and may no longer be valid. The views expressed in this work are solely those of the author and do not necessarily reflect the views of the publisher, and the publisher hereby disclaims any responsibility for them.

ISBN: 978-1-4502-7903-1 (sc)
ISBN: 978-1-4502-7902-4 (ebook)

Printed in the United States of America

iUniverse rev. date: 4/5/2011

Dedication

In Loving Memory of My Mother
Johnnie Mary Carter
"To God Be the Glory"

Acknowledgments

All scripture references were taken from the King James Version of the Bible.

I would like to thank the following people for their help and support while I was on the journey with my Ladybug.

Sam, my younger brother, for being there for me every time I called; you were my backbone and my Mr. Dependable,

Beverly, Nel and Danielle for standing by me; without you I would not have been able to make it,

Dr. Amos C. Johnson, MD, Farmington Hills Internal Medicine, who kept me on my feet,

My co-workers at Blue Cross Blue Shield of Michigan for their understanding and support as I tried to work and cope,

The Burnette Baptist Church family for your prayers and support,

The FOCUS Hospices organization and especially Barbara, the Chaplain that was so helpful to the very end,

Dr. Zakari Tata, MD, Home Health Care provider,

Elijah Ngugi for helping with the back cover.
And finally, many thanks to the ladies at Bible Study Fellowship, International in Plymouth, for your prayers and support.

Table of Contents

Acknowledgments	vii
Foreword	xiii
Preface	xv
Introduction	xvii

Chapter 1   Childhood to Widowhood 1
Miraculous Rescue 2
Married Life 6
Missed Opportunities 8
Widowed Suddenly 1953 9
The move to Detroit Michigan in 1953 12

Chapter 2   A Difficult Life 14
First Child Left 1960 18
Last Child Left 1972 19
Housemate 21

Chapter 3   Expected and Unexpected Changes 23
Always Mother's Child 28
Medical Problems Intensified 34

Chapter 4   Dementia Emerges Unexpectedly 36
Back Surgery in 1995 36
The Battles Begin 37
Home after Back Surgery in 1995 40
Hospital Emergency 41
Fear of the Dark 42
Driving Becomes a Problem 45
Red Flags of Memory Loss 48

Chapter 5   More Serious Illness   51
   Triple Bypass Surgery   51
   Dreaded Confusion Returns   54
   Big Surprise   60
   Immediate Needs Met   61

Chapter 6   Many Faces of Alzheimer   63
   Caregivers for Ladybug   63
   Independent Again   64
   Rehabilitation   65
   Turning Point   68
   Confused Speech   69
   Constant Motion   71
   Silent and Combative   73
   Adult Protective Services   75

Chapter 7   Connections with the Past   77
   Traveling Attitude   78
   Unexpected Fear   79
   Disturbing Reunion   81
   Surprise from the Past   83
   Second Time Around   85
   Hometown Visit   86

Chapter 8   The Joys and Pains of Care Giving   89
   Care Giving on the Road   89
   Care Giving Shared   90
   Dishonest Caregivers   93
   Crafty Mind   94
   Respite Care   98

Chapter 9   Alzheimer's Disease Fast Forward   101
   In Another World   104
   Substitute Children   105
   Moving On   107

Sympathetic Observers	111
Chapter 10 Guardian Angels and New Adventures	113
Out of Control	114
Embarrassing Incidents	116
Flashbacks	119
Mysterious Visits to the Police Precinct	120
Grocery Shopping	122
Adventures at Meal Time	123
Communication Problems	126
Chapter 11 Challenging Adventures	129
Searching for Her Children	129
Caught by Surprise	134
An Unexpected Standoff	137
Locked Out	139
Church Service Disruptions	140
Chapter 12 Frightening Experiences and Complicated Decisions	144
Swallowed Sewing Needles	145
Shocking Hospital Experience	147
Retirement	151
A Major Emergency	153
Tough Decision and Horrendous Experiences	155
Chapter 13 Last Mile of the Way	159
Lack of Compassion	159
New Experiences in Care Giving	161
Recognition of Special Days	163
Show of Emotions	164
New Relationships Formed	165
Emergencies	166

Hospice Care	172
Answer to the Congestion Problem	172
Chapter 14 End of Journey	176
Chapter 15 The Epilogue	178

Foreword

By Dr. Fredie B. Carter-Bonner

Aging baby boomers are becoming very concerned about the escalation of Alzheimer's disease. A number of them are currently caring for loved ones stricken with the disease and do not know exactly what to expect. The National Institute on Aging Report of April 20, 2010 states that over 5 million Americans have Alzheimer's.

Ruthie D. Carter's book, *My Ladybug's Alzheimer's Journey*, is a timely resource for persons who have been diagnosed with the disease and for persons attending loved ones with the disease. This book is also intended for those individuals who serve others and show mercy with cheerfulness in the performance of their responsibilities. Ms. Carter chronicled her mother's illness with dementia for over twelve years.

In her book, *My Ladybug's Alzheimer's Journey*, Ms. Carter shows how important it is to share symptoms noted in a loved one with other family members. She kept her family informed, and it helped them to face issues reasonably and more calmly. Also, getting an early diagnosis of her mother's illness helped the family make informed decisions.

Ms. Carter has chosen to share experiences of caring for her mother who struggled with Alzheimer's disease for twelve years and eleven months. Ms. Carter's book, *My Ladybug's Alzheimer's Journey*, will be inspirational and helpful to persons trying to make decisions about the care of loved ones with the Alzheimer's disease or any illness.

Chapters in the book give us insights of real people dealing with real issues. There are times when your heart will fill with joy. Other times, your eyes may swell with tears. During other times, you will find yourself smiling at normal everyday experiences.

While Alzheimer's may affect people stricken with the disease differently, some of the experiences in this book may be similar to the ones you are experiencing or you will experience. Hopefully, reading this book will help lessen the burden of caring for a family member who has Alzheimer's.

My Ladybug's Alzheimer's Journey by Ruthie D. Carter offers a compelling story laced with a daughter's love for her mother. It is a reflection of Ms. Carter's' spirituality and her never fading trust in God…Her portrayal of her mother, brothers and other persons in her life is authentic and establishes caring relationships as shown by the name Ladybug, a name of endearment for her mother.

Dr. Fredie Carter-Bonner is a writer, educational consultant and a retired principal who resides in Detroit, Michigan.

Preface

My Ladybug's Alzheimer's Journey is being shared to honor caregivers past, present and future that accepted and will accept the responsibility of caring for a parent, child, relative, a friend or a patient during a period of disability or illness. It also includes eighty percent of nursing home workers, doctors, nurses, social workers and other professions who have dedicated their lives to serve the disabled.

It is especially for those who have been diagnosed with debilitating diseases that will lead to their dependence on another person for their needs in the future. Hopefully, they will have the opportunity to plan for that time in their lives and prayerfully select individuals with the gift of service as defined in Romans 12, to entrust with their care.

My Ladybug's Alzheimer's Journey is also intended for those individuals who serve others and show compassion, mercy and patience in the performance of their responsibilities. I have come to realize that it takes a special type of individual to devote his or her life unselfishly to the health and well being of others. We are blessed when we come across such persons. For not all who are employed in those special positions are anointed to perform the services needed.

No one person can take care of the needs of a person with special needs. It takes a society that is sensitive to the needs of the disabled and elderly. Just as the familiar ancient African proverb states, "It takes a whole village to raise a child," basically it takes a village to take care of an ill person. It does not matter whether the illness is physical or mental, the needs are the same.

I thank God that I live in a country where some levels of the required services are provided for the welfare of all its citizens. I have come to understand the physical and emotional sacrifices that must be endured in the course of caring for incapacitated individuals, whether out of love or a sense of duty. For this, I will be eternally grateful to God. I also understand that God works through those whom he prepares to serve others, and He will provide for those who love Him.

Introduction

My Ladybug's Alzheimer's Journey reveals the struggles of a mother with the disease and her daughter that leads to a paradoxical reversal of roles where the daughter becomes the mother and the mother becomes the child.

My Ladybug's Alzheimer's Journey deals with the devastating impact the dreadful disease has on the lives of both the mother and daughter. The debilitating disease strikes without warning and takes over the mother's existence in all phases of her life. In reality it shakes the emotional foundation which is based upon the love of the daughter toward her mother. It is even more agonizing when she watches her mother drifting away, disappearing into a world of disorientation and delirium. She looks like her mother, but she does not act like her mother.

My Ladybug's Alzheimer's Journey will prepare those who have not experienced such unusual realities and not catch them by surprise like me when my mother encountered the difficulties of this mysterious disease. I also hope it will support and encourage those who are experiencing the burdens of loss of a parent or loved one in the strange world of disorientation and aggressive behavior of Alzheimer's disease

My Ladybug's Alzheimer's Journey shares background and high points of the devastating changes that occurred in my mother that took her from being my mother to someone I did not recognize as my mother and finally to someone that was other than my mother. In the beginning she was my mother acting out of character, and then she became a mischievous stranger and finally my child. My mother was searching for her children and I was searching for my mother.

These are true experiences that I encountered while taking care of my mother for twelve years and eleven months while she struggled with the mysterious Alzheimer's disease. Hopefully, it will be inspirational and helpful to persons trying to make difficult decisions about the care of loved one with the disease. The intent is also to prepare caregivers for some of the unusual realities that may change the behavior of patients and loved ones.

On October 9, 2003, when my mother was brought home from a three-week stay in a nursing home, I was inspired to document events that had occurred and were occurring as a result of her struggle with Alzheimer's disease. She was first diagnosed with dementia in March of 1995, and it ended with her death on February 24, 2008. She had lived with me since August 1985, and I made the difficult decision of taking care of her in the home she recognized and loved, no matter her condition. Primarily because she had always wanted her own home and had been unable to afford one.

My Ladybug's Alzheimer's Journey

Ladybug's journey actually began long before she was diagnosed with Alzheimer's disease. In fact, I think the circumstances surrounding her early childhood, in a small rural town in southern Georgia, could be related to her journey. I felt it was important to use those circumstances as a starting point. It is my uneducated opinion that the loss of her mother and close relatives in a short span of time during her early years, contributed to irreversible emotional problems.

It is not my intent to convey the impression that the entire twelve years and eleven months, after my mother was diagnosed with Alzheimer's disease, were filled with extraordinary events. The truth is just the opposite. There were many days when nothing out of the ordinary happened. Therefore, I will not spend time giving day by day accounts of those days and events in her life. I will deal mostly with the experiences that were unusual and that caused our lives to be filled with catastrophes and uncertainties.

As you have probably guessed, Ladybug was my endearing name for my mother. I had called her Ma Dea all of my life, but when she started to act out behaviors under the influence of the Alzheimer's disease, she was no longer Ma Dea. It just did not seem right calling her Ma Dea when she did not recognize it coming from me as an adult. My clue while on *My Ladybug's Alzheimer's Journey* was that she was always searching for her small children and they called her Ma Dea.

While sitting next to her bed in the hospital following a near death experience, I had time to think about her life at length and the struggles she had gone through to get to be my Ma Dea. I remembered the sacrifices she made to rear my two brothers and me after my father's death in 1953. That is when God elevated my understanding and love for my mother to a different level. It was after that revelation that every moment I was able to take care of her became a joy and not a burden. She became my Ladybug sometime after that moment in time. I am not sure when it first surfaced and where it came from, but one day I found myself calling her Ladybug. It worked for both of us and it remained the name I called her until her death.

My prayers are that *My Ladybug's Alzheimer's Journey* will encourage and strengthen others who are on a journey with loved ones who have been diagnosed with Alzheimer's disease and other debilitating diseases. *My Ladybug's Alzheimer's Journey* is not intended to be a manual of instructions, only a level of sharing that will allow other to make the best possible decision for them and their loved ones. Some may decide to put their loved ones in facilities equipped to deal with their special needs and others may decide as I did to take care of their loved one at home. I have no advice to offer as to what the decision should be because it will vary with individual circumstances. I only have my experiences to share.

For those who are faced with the challenge, it is recommended that the Alzheimer's Association and other Senior Care Agencies be contacted for help. These and other organizations will be valuable in making the appropriate decision.

It is also my hope that *My Ladybug's Alzheimer's Journey* may be useful as a case study in training caregivers and in research to better understand the cause of certain behavior in Alzheimer's patients. Support groups could also draw from my coping experiences in the care of Ladybug.

In the latter stages of *My Ladybug's Alzheimer's Journey*, I was invited to a Bible Study Group called Bible Study Fellow, International, by a dear friend. The study of the Gospel of Matthews and the prayers of that group of ladies gave me the courage to face the challenges that eventually lead to the end of my Ladybug's life.

So for clarity sake, I will often refer to my mother as Ma Dea first and then Ladybug. My brothers will be called my older brother and my younger brother. Other relatives, caregivers, friends and the medical team that shared the journey will simply be referred to by those titles.

Chapter 1
Childhood to Widowhood

Ma Dea never knew the exact date of her birth. The birth date she celebrated was September 19, 1923. However, she had no birth certificate to validate that date. She was not sure where the information came from, but grew up believing that she was born to Johnny and Estelle Cobbitt in Americus, Georgia on the birth date she celebrated. Ma Dea was orphaned as a toddler and had no memory of her biological parents or the town of her birth. She was the youngest and only girl out of five children born to her mother.

Ma Dea's brothers were the source of the limited information she knew about her family. They remembered that their mother, grandmother and aunt all perished in an epidemic believed to be tuberculosis because the furniture and bedding was burned after each death. The birth date my mother celebrated was questioned by one of her brothers later in her adult life. He remembered her birth to be in April, but the new information could not be verified. When their mother died, the five children were left motherless and homeless.

My mother was given her father's surname, but that was really all she knew about him. She had no memory of her father or his family. Unfortunately, as far as she knew, no one had been able to locate him after her mother passed away. That bothered Ma Dea, especially later in her life. She longed for recognition of who she was and searched for news about her family. She often watched television programs about people finding lost love ones and fantasized about her father finding her after years of searching. She urged me to search the internet for information about her father and his family. The searches never produced any information to substantiate the information she had been given relating to her family. It became clear that the information she had been given was not accurate.

One of Ma Dea's brothers shared a different version of her origin and how she came to live with the cousins. He told her that her father was a lumberjack and had worked in a logging camp. He had left the two younger children with a cousin after their mother's death, with the intent of returning for them. However, he believed that there was an accident and my mother's father was killed. Like other information she obtained, that account came when my mother was up in age, and it could not be verified and it contradicted what she had been told originally. The aged cousin that raised my mother had never shared that information with her, so it probably was also incorrect.

Miraculous Rescue

Ma Dea's earliest memories were when she was two or three years old. She remembered being locked in a closet with other children in the small southern town where she lived. She recalled wearing only overalls and no shoes on the cold winter day. The adult son of her cousin and local authorities broke down the closet door to rescue her and her youngest brother when they heard a child crying. She had no memory of why they were locked in the closet. She was later told that they lived in the poor section of Americus Georgia and it was believed that the more children a family had, the more hands were available to work in the fields gathering the crops during the pre Great Depression era. Apparently the people were aware that the two small children were orphans and wanted to keep them for whatever reasons.

The cousins took Ma Dea and her brother to live with them in the country. The three older brothers were later discovered living on the streets in Americus and also brought to join their siblings in the home of the cousins. My mother remembered her cousins as being a middle-aged couple. They did not have much, but were known for sharing what they had with homeless children of relatives. The three oldest boys only stayed with the cousins a short while. They were anxious to be independent and eventually ran away. My mother and her youngest brother were left behind with the cousin and her husband. The living arrangements were common during the 1920's and 1930's in the south.

My Mother remembered the house she grew up in as a large rambling wood framed house that sat in the middle of the open countryside. It had a large front yard and pecan orchards on the side. One of her chores was to sweep the large yard free of trash and debris. The evenings in the country were dark, but millions of stars illuminated the sky. The fascinating night sounds of crickets chirping and the various frog sounds could be heard in the distance as the children made a game of trying to catch the colorful fireflies.

Ma Dea had fond memories of the cousins and their home. Their children were all adults, but the house was always filled with children they were in the process of rearing. There was a continuous mix of grand children and cousins that had also been taken in during the time Ma Dea and her brother lived in the home. Her brother was unhappy working in the fields doing day labor because the work was hard and the pay was minimal. He ran away the first opportunity he found and joined an older brother who had settled in Florida for a time. That left my mother alone with the cousins and other children. Her brothers did not come back to visit her often enough for a close relationship to develop between them during her early years. However, they bonded later in life as adults.

The family that Ma Dea lived with was very poor but times grew harder during the Great Depression in the 1930's and early 1940's. She had very few possessions, but had enough food to eat and clean clothes to wear. Her surrogate mother had a large capacity for love that was shared freely and my mother loved her. She remembered her as a warm fair skinned pleasantly plump woman who always wore a clean apron. When Ma Dea cried her tears were often dried with the apron.

As children, we loved hearing about Ma Dea's childhood and stories about the people who lived in the large country house. She cherished the memories and enjoyed sharing them with us and our friends. Some of the children in the house presented sibling rivalry situations and my mother's actions during the early stages of the dementia suggested that she had to fight to survive in some situations much the same way as with siblings. She was especially close to one of the granddaughters. She always thought of her as a sister.

My mother attended a one room country school during the early part of her life. One teacher taught all grade levels in the same room. She had to walk miles to get to school, but she loved her school day experiences and used them to encourage us when we were growing up. Ma Dea was a slow learner and only stayed in school through the eighth grade because the school was not equipped to give her the special help she needed.

Ma Dea had grown to her full height of five feet, five which was tall for girls. She was thin, but loved playing basketball with the boy's basketball team. She recalled wearing her cousin's high top tennis shoes that had to be tied around her ankles and the toes flopped as she ran up and down the basketball court. She had worked to earn money for new tennis shoes, but her cousin's husband had spent the money on something else.

One other treasured childhood memory was attending church on Sundays. Ma Dea loved church and found comfort in attending the worship services on Sunday and various revival meetings during the week. She also enjoyed the times when her cousin read the Bible to her in the evenings. As she grew older, she drifted to a denomination different than that of her cousins but always maintained her strong faith in God.

Married Life

Ma Dea met and married my father, a farmer, at the age of seventeen in 1940, over a year and a half before the bombing of Pearl Harbor. She remembered that she was slightly afraid of the tall dark handsome young man when she first met him. In contrast, Ma Dea was a tall, slim pretty young woman and they made a handsome young couple. He was twenty years old and lived at home with his mother and siblings. The couple had a simple wedding and moved in with his family until they were able to move into their own home. Her mother-in-law intimidated my mother, but she loved her husband's younger brothers and sisters.

World War II broke out in 1941, and my father was drafted, but was rejected for a reason that was unclear. After getting over the scare of his having to go to war, they moved to their own house. Their first home was a small one bedroom wood framed farm house near a wooded area and sat across the road from a larger house occupied by the adult daughter of the cousin that had reared Ma Dea. She had not learned to be a home maker while growing up with her cousins and had to be taught how to take care of the house. But In spite of having to learn to be a home maker, my mother remembered that period in her life as being the happiest she had ever been. She loved being lady of the house.

Ma Dea always remembered that her husband loved her and patiently taught her how to be a wife and home maker. Although he was only three years older, he was mature beyond his years because of family responsibilities. My older brother and I were born in the one bedroom farm house. My mother finally felt like she had found the special love that she was so desperately seeking. Her young husband gave her life stability and she clung to him with a child like dependency.

They later found a larger house to accommodate their growing family and moved miles away from their relatives. Ma Dea missed her cousins and was sometimes unreasonable when she could not visit her surrogate parents and the home she remembered. She would resort to temper tantrums in order to get what she wanted. She conveyed that our father was just the opposite and their personalities complemented each other. When her husband could not take her back home for one reason or another, Ma Dea would become very angry and tearful.

My mother was apparently accustomed to having her way and when she did not get it she would become very emotional. When the tantrums failed, she would respond by packing our things and getting one of the neighbors to take her where she wanted to go. We remembered as children that Ma Dea would sometimes get a neighbor to take her home when our farther could not make the trip. However, on Sunday evenings when she would see the car coming down the road, she would say to us, *"Get your things together, here comes your daddy."* When he stopped the car, we would climb in as if nothing unusual had happened, and he would take us home again. Looking back, I guess that is where I eventually learned to cope with my mother's hysteria and tantrums.

In spite of her actions, Ma Dea loved her home. She loved the way the house sat back off the country dirt road. The barns and storage buildings hid the house from the road for privacy. The area in front of the house had been fenced in and the family played softball and other games there on holidays and other family gatherings. Beyond the fenced area was a stream that ran through the property and off into the wooded area beyond. Once a year when the water was unusually low, neighbors came and they would catch the fish in steel drums. It was a festive occasion and there would be a fish fry and children for us to play with. Ma Dea loved entertaining.

Missed Opportunities

Ma Dea missed out on opportunities to grow and develop emotionally due to no fault of her own. For unknown reasons, she was not taught responsibilities like how to care for a home which is a natural developmental progression for girls. For instance not knowing how to cook and keep house were handicaps she had to overcome before she could be a good wife and mother. There could have been many reasons for not teaching her those skills. One could have been that she was the poor little cousin without family and she needed to be protected. Another reason could have been that having no mother, the natural curiosity of learning to be like her mother was absent.

My mother's lack of emotional development as a child caused her to miss out on other opportunities for growth and development. For example she opted to let her husband take full responsibility for managing the family's resources. There were important skills required for independent farmers to be successful in the late forties and early fifties. Money management skills were essential for success as a farmer. Planning and budgeting were key factors in having enough resources to last for twelve months. Crops were harvested and sold once a year and out of the profits, bills had to paid, seed purchased for new crops, clothing for the family, some food had to be grown and purchased, and money had to be saved for the future and emergencies.

Ma Dea was allowed to exist in a dream world free of responsibilities in both situations. She was perfectly happy being provided for as a child and an adult. However the consequences of her not participating in the adult responsibilities for the family caused her irreparable emotional damage. Again the reasons for her not participating in those areas could come under the heading of love and protection, but nevertheless, the emotional costs were so great, it was very difficult for her to recover. There was no way of her knowing that the husband she depended on would be with her for such a short period of time. She paid dearly for failing to take advantage of learning the second set of responsibilities as an adult.

Widowed Suddenly 1953

Ma Dea only shared with us the happy memories of her married life. I am not sure she even remembered the unhappy experiences. She was perfectly happy most of the time and totally dependent on my father for all of her needs. He was head of the family and made all decisions and provisions for the family. They had always wanted to have more children. However, there was a hiatus of nine years and ten months after the first two children were born. The long awaited third child arrived on May 6, 1952. The family was excited about the birth of the baby. Life was good for my mother during that time.

Tragic struck and changed the course of Ma Dea's life forever on August 12, 1953, only fifteen short months after the birth of the new baby. Her happy life ended abruptly late one summer afternoon in southern Georgia, after only thirteen years of marriage. Her husband died suddenly at the age of thirty three. He was ill only two weeks and was suddenly gone. She was devastated at the loss. She grieved profusely over his death. My mother was forced into instant maturity and it did not fit her very well. Her aging cousin came to live with us to help her adjust and my mother leaned heavily on her for support. Ma Dea had to step into the leadership role of the family without time for on the job training.

During their marriage, my mother and father made vows that they would not remarry if anything happened to disrupt their lives together before their children were out on their own. The vows were made because of the rumors about incest and child molestation that were rampant during that time. However, my father released Ma Dea from that promise when he realized that he was going to precede her in death. He even called us to his bedside one day when we were complaining about what she had prepared for breakfast. He told us, *"Eat what your mother fixes for you to eat because sometimes she might not have anything else."* My father must have known that times would not be easy for his young wife after he was gone, and he wanted to help her as much as possible.

Ma Dea chose to honor the vow she had made to my father, in spite of his wishes for her life after his death. She was an attractive young widow and could have remarried and had a good life, but she devoted her life to child rearing. She was shy, but a strikingly beautiful young woman with fair skin and long legs nearing her thirtieth birthday when my father died. My mother had never weighed more than 120 pounds until her mid fifties. And, although she was forced to purchase most of her clothes from the Goodwill after my father's death, she had a good eye for fashions and was a good dresser.

My mother's oldest brother mysteriously appeared a few days after the burial of my father. We had heard stories about him but had never met him before that time. My older brother and I were at the well pumping water when we saw him approaching us. We both recognized him from the stories Ma Dea told us about him just appearing unexpectedly. He stayed to help Ma Dea with gathering and selling the crops and disposing of the farm equipment, but he was known for not remaining in one place for any length of time. Ma Dea could not depend on him to stay and help her with the farm. By definition, I think the term for my wandering uncle was a "hobo".

Cousins encouraged Ma Dea to move to Detroit where her brothers lived. They were her closest relatives and would be willing to help her with her children. She cried over the advice because she wanted to move back with the cousins who had taken her in as a child. However, that was not an option available to her at that time. My mother was not alone anymore, she had three children. Besides, the cousins were retired and their granddaughter and her family took care of them.

The move to Detroit Michigan in 1953

Moving to a strange cold city three short months after her husband's death was the last thing Ma Dea wanted to do. However, she did not have any other choice. The cousins who reared her were up in age and unable to help. Her brothers and their wives in Detroit were almost strangers to her, but had the resources to help with her family. Although she had visited her brothers in Detroit several times, no close relationships or bonds were formed during those visits. She had lived on a farm most of her life and had nothing in common with her city relatives. But, she could not work the farm on her own. She sold everything, settled debts and took what money that was left and moved her family to Detroit.

The move was very hard on Ma Dea and her young grief stricken family. We were a family in a crisis crying out for help. We were all still grieving for my father, but Ma Dea was hurting the most. She was unprepared for the challenges her new life brought. Sometime she would cry for hours at a time and we were at a loss as how to console her. Her brothers and their wives were helpful but did not provide the continuous support and nurturing she needed.

My mother had always depended on my father to take care of the family business, so she had very little experience in making important decisions and the process frustrated her. She trustingly gave what money she had left to one of her brothers under the impression that he would provide a place for her family to live. Her lack of knowledge and experience in taking the leadership role in taking care of the family left Ma Dea open to be taken advantage of by her brother.

Ma Dea moved upstairs above the brother to whom she had given the money. My uncle was a single man and did not provide the moral support my mother required so desperately. He did not adapt to the role of advisor and mentor to her or her children. She was in a strange cold place and had no idea how to provide for her young family. She had lived there less than a year when he told her that she needed to be out on her own with her children.

Chapter 2
A Difficult Life

In the early fifties the automobile industry was thriving in Detroit. Working on the assembly line of one of the automobile companies would have provided enough money to pay for a babysitter and take care of Ma Dea's family. However, transportation prevented her from taking advantage of those employment opportunities. The only other employment available to Ma Dea was day work in private homes. She tried the day work but the pay was not enough to pay for a babysitter and the other expenses to take of her family. Her three children, ages thirteen, eleven and eighteen months were depending on her for survival. And her brothers grew tired of trying to help Ma Dea solve her problems.

My mother had no money left, so her youngest brother helped her find a room in a rooming house. He paid the rent for the first month and the four of us moved into the one bedroom with kitchen privileges. God touched the heart of the landlady who was an alcoholic. She provided food for us after we had eaten our last loaf of bread. Ma Dea told us, *"This is our last loaf of bread; we are going to eat it, say our prayers and go to bed."* The next morning the landlady knocked on the door of our room and told Ma Dea that there was food for us on the table in the kitchen. My mother got us up and dressed for school, and we went downstairs to find a large box of groceries waiting for us. We knew for sure that God answered our prayers.

Ma Dea did not know where she would get food for us after that, but she believed that the Lord would provide for us as he said in Hebrews 13:5b, "…for he hath said, I will never leave thee, nor forsake thee." God continued to watch over us. One day after school one of my new friends invited me over to her home. I guess her mother noticed that I was not properly dressed for the cold weather. We did not need heavy coats and boots in the South. Therefore, we had none of those items. My friend's mother told me to bring my mother over to meet her. She took Ma Dea to places where she could apply for help and get food and clothing for us in the interim. We were introduced to second hand clothes for the first time. The clothes were used, but they were clean and warm.

Another positive thing in our new city life was that my older brother found a church that reminded him of the church we had left in the South. My mother took the family the very next Sunday, and we indeed had found a church home where the people were friendly and supportive. Ma Dea met a friend at the church that took her under her wings and taught her about city life. Life was still lonely but better for us. With the help of God, her new found friends and the Aid to Dependent Children, Ma Dea was able to keep us together. She was adamant about us growing up together because of the separation of her siblings.

Ma Dea was a good mother to us although she was a strict disciplinarian. Looking back, the discipline was always mixed with love. We did not understand it at the time, but she believed in using the Bible as her guide for rearing us. The scripture she used most was Proverbs 13:24, which says, "He that spareth his rod hateth his son; but he that loveth him chasteneth him betimes." So, punishment was given out equally to sons and daughter. Her teachings are what her three children live by today.

My mother always tried to set good examples for us to follow. She took us to church every Sunday where we attended Sunday school and participated in youth auxiliaries. We were taught to love and develop personal relationships with Jesus Christ. She also taught us how to take care of ourselves because she would say, "*I may not always be with you.*" It would frighten us when she talked like that, because we had already lost our father. We didn't want to think about losing our mother. Most of all, she taught us to love and look out for one another.

There wasn't much money left out of the monthly Aid to Dependent Children check for entertainment, so after homework was finished, Ma Dea would play games with us or we watched the small second hand black and white television she had been able to purchase. She insisted that we stay in school and get a good education so homework always came first. She wanted us to have all of the advantages she never had in life. I can remember near the end of the month, sometimes all we had to eat was potatoes and hotdogs, but we were never hungry. We loved French fries, home fries, mashed potatoes, baked potatoes and basically potatoes any way.

Holidays were lonely and sad for our little family without its head. On Sunday afternoons when there was no church, we would sit and eat treats Ma Dea cooked and shared memories of the family gatherings at our farm house in the rural South when we were young. The stories fascinated my younger brother, because he had no memories of his father or life in the country. He was only fifteen months old when our father died. Other times Ma Dea would make sandwiches and we would ride the bus to the end of the line, get off and walk around, eat our sandwiches, and get back on the bus for the ride home.

Our favorite excursions were to the Public Library to look at books Ma Dea could not afford to buy or the Art Museum and look at exhibits and paintings. When she had extra money we would ride the street car on Woodward Avenue downtown to the J. L. Hudson's department store. We liked the smells of perfume and newness. We would ride the elevator from floor to floor being careful to respect the uniformed elevator operators. We never had money to buy anything, but we enjoyed seeing the toys and new clothes. Afterwards we would go to the S.S. Kresge's 5 and 10 Cent store across the street for lunch in the basement. The name of the store was changed to Kmart in the early sixties. The Sam's department store on Randolph Street is where clothes were purchased for the family. Special treats were when one of our uncles would invite us to picnics sponsored by the UAW. Everything was free, and Ma Dea had as much fun as we did.

First Child Left 1960

I was the second child and only girl, however, I was the first to leave home a year after graduating from high school. I joined the military over Ma Dea's objections, but she finally gave in and signed the papers giving her consent. My two brothers were still at home, and I wrote and called home often. I also made it a practice to send gifts and extra money for special days to make things better for them while I was away.

When I returned from the military, my older brother had gotten married and moved out to start his own family. My mother insisted that I move in with her and my younger brother when my original plans for leaving the city fell through. It was a very difficult decision for me, because I was no longer the submissive teenager that she remembered. I finally relented and moved back home with my mother. I soon learned that Ma Dea had a hidden agenda for me moving in with her and my younger brother. There were nine years and ten months between my younger brother and me, and he was still in middle school. I did not know it, but my mother had decided that it was her time to enjoy life, and my time to stay home with my younger brother. That was totally out of character for her, and I was a little surprised but went along with her plan. I consented because I remembered the sacrifices she had made after my father's death and felt she deserved some happiness.

Before I could change my mind about staying with them, Ma Dea found a larger house for us to live in without any input from me. It was a single family home on a busy street with three bedrooms which she could not afford without my help. I settled in and made myself content. That living arrangement worked for more than ten years. It ended when the house was put on the market and sold. Ma Dea wanted me to buy it, but I was not interested in becoming the owner of that particular house under those conditions. When the house sold, she rushed out to find a new home for us. In her haste, she signed a lease for a flat that had only two bedrooms. There was no bedroom for me. That gave me the opportunity to get my own apartment. Ma Dea and my younger brother moved into their new home alone.

Last Child Left 1972

When my youngest brother graduated from college, he was anxious to be independent. He found a job and moved out of the house with Ma Dea. She protested but finally accepted that all three of her children had grown up and were living separate lives. We all had good jobs and she was happy about that. She only had a little while to adjust to her youngest child leaving home before he moved to another city. She had accepted the fact that he was no longer at home because he lived nearby and visited her often. However, she was very unhappy when the baby of the family accepted a job in another city and moved. We thought it was a sad day when he left home, but when he left the city my mother was overwhelmed. For the first time since my father's death, she was left all alone with only the family pet for company.

Ma Dea had no companionship because she formed no lasting relationships outside of church. She had not made a life for herself independent of her children. As a result, when my younger brother left the city and was not in and out of her house, it had more of a staggering impact on her life than anyone realized. She had devoted her life to her children and had an innate desire to control their lives even though they were adults.

Each one of us had to develop our own coping mechanisms for dealing with Ma Dea's desire to manage our lives:

- The first born would leave when Ma Dea started to tell him how to live his life. That would aggravate her and she would start to fuss and yell, but he would not stop to listen. One day she followed him out into the street and stood in front of the car to prevent him from moving the car. Then she proceeded to shout out what she had to tell him for the whole neighborhood to hear.
- The middle child initially listened quietly until it became unbearable. Then she tried the tactics of the first born without success. Ma Dea would wait for her to reach home and call and yell and scream over the telephone. It would go on and on. Finally she tried not answering the telephone. That was countered with Ma Dea coming over to see why she was not answering.
- The youngest child was from a different generation and had his own unique way of dealing with Ma Dea's form of discipline. He would yell back which infuriated her more. One day she took the broom to him even though he was in his twenties.

We all understood that Ma Dea was lonely and unhappy and needed to vent her frustrations the only way she knew. It was evident that she loved us and missed her mothering responsibilities. However, we were at a loss as how to help her.

Housemate

Ma Dea finally found a woman at church that needed a place to live after a while. That was perfect because she was not only company for her, she shared the living expenses. That arrangement worked successfully for a few years before my mother started complaining about her housemate. I had also noticed other changes in my mother's personality. At first, I thought she was still going through a delayed empty nest syndrome; of course I had no clue as to what was really happening in her mind. She refused to talk about it with me or listen to my suggestions.

My visits usually ended in her being upset with me for one reason or another. I really got concerned when I began to notice things out of the ordinary like there would be no food in the refrigerator and bills were left lying around unpaid. It also became very difficult for her to relate to other people. The relationship with her landlady, who lived upstairs above them, deteriorated to the point she asked Ma Dea to move. The message was very clear when her housemate was allowed to stay in the house

I prayed for a solution to this dilemma as Ma Dea began to look for a new place to live. A senior citizen apartment was not an option she would consider. I was uncomfortable with her living alone in any other arrangement. She had always wanted a home of her own where she could plant flowers and a vegetable garden. So, the only solution was to purchase a house and make a home together. That way she would not be alone.

My mother had all kind of objections to the solution. She did not want to feel accountable to anyone. She didn't have a problem with me living with her, and I explained that there was no difference in the two scenarios. After many discussions, we finally came up with living arrangements that would meet both of our needs. It was very difficult for her, because she was the mother and felt she should be the provider and not have someone provide for her needs. Ma Dea was head of the household in her mind and she was not going to relinquish her authority. She had to be convinced that she would operate as the head of her home.

Chapter 3
Expected and Unexpected Changes

To expedite the search for a house to buy, I did not include Ma Dea in the decision on which house I would buy. I found a three bedroom bungalow that allowed both of us to have privacy, in a quiet neighborhood and made an offer. The offer was accepted and the deal was closed. When it was time to move in, our agreed upon living arrangements were in trouble from the beginning. I was not prepared for the additional compromises I would have to make to satisfy Ma Dea. In trying to make sure my mother was happy I neglected to take into consideration my own needs and the role I would ultimately have to play in the home.

We ran into our first encounter when we went furniture shopping. It never occurred to me that Ma Dea would want to bring her assortment of furniture to our new home. I was saved on some pieces because they were too large and would not fit. She insisted on bringing all of her old furniture although some had to be stored in the basement. The sofa she insisted on putting in the living room had large red roses and did not match anything else in the room. However, it was too large to fit through any doors of the house. She would not give up; she had to saw the legs off to get it through the door, but with the help of the movers, she managed to get it in the house. The men were amazed at her tenacity. We finally agreed to put the sofa with the sawed off legs in the family room until it could be replaced.

I should not have been surprised because our mother daughter relationship had never been a healthy one. I had read extensively on the subject and had finally come to the conclusion that we did not fit any of the models and I was on my own. After I realized that Ma Dea was having problems and unable to adjust, I had to go the extra mile to keep peace and harmony. I had to assess my own needs and made a decision on what I was willing to give up in order for us to live together, even though I was bearing the expenses.

The lesson was hard, but I learned that going the extra mile is something caregivers must be willing to do when working with loved ones who are incapacitated in any way. I made many mistakes that were stressful for both of us before the lesson was learned. The demands on my time were disruptive and made me feel overwhelmed until I came to grips with what was expected of me in our arrangement.

Ma Dea was rarely happy the first years we lived together. She had already started to live in the past and my efforts to assess, evaluate and improve the situation were inadequate. The first Christmas we shared under the same roof was a nightmare. I tried to make it the best Christmas ever and failed miserably. She did not like anything I had done for the holidays. I bought new decorations and a live tree and put Christmas lights outside on the hedges and around the house. She was upset and at first I had no idea what was wrong. When she finally told me that I had left her out of Christmas, I could have cried. All she wanted was her old decorations that she had accumulated over the years. After that first Christmas, I packed up the new decorations and put them in the basement to stay. I decided to let her take the lead in decorating the home for holidays and only did the things she asked me to complete.

It occurred to me that the odd mix of Christmas decorations Ma Dea had accumulated over the years were very dear to her and in her eyes irreplaceable. It did not matter how she had obtained the mishmash of decorations. The important thing was that each one was a treasured possession. She never threw anything away unless it was broken and could not be fixed. Rather, she carefully packed away every piece year after year. Every piece of decoration held special memories of how she had been able to survive and provide for her children.

The solution to the problem was that I had to be more sensitive to Ma Dea's needs and learn to avoid changes in her life. It was the mid eighties when I first observed the changes in my mother. I had heard of senility, but never Alzheimer's disease. Education awareness of the disease would have helped in making decisions that would govern both of our lives. My lack of knowledge is the only excuse I can come up with for not identifying some critical problem areas.

From experience, it is a red flag when loved ones show unusual changes in character. Ma Dea's unusual attachment to things from the past was out of the ordinary or rather I had not noticed it before. If I had not ignored obvious symptoms that something was wrong, maybe I could have found a way to reduce some of the pain. It could be something as simple as a change in medication, but it is wise to seek advice from a professional. Be it, the family doctor or another relative. Two heads are always better than one. It does not have to be a big production.

It did not matter to Ma Dea that there was very little money when we were growing up on Aid to Dependent Children and now we all had jobs and were able to afford more. My pride in being able to provide shiny new things to replace the old ones did not produce the happiness I had hoped for. She had learned how to take what little she had and make it into something special and that was more important to her. The most valuable lesson I learned that first Christmas was that my mother was living in the past and that I should not make unnecessary changes in her surroundings. Her new home became her old home in every way possible.

What I did not know was that change in the lives of elder relatives can cause confusion and bring about strange behaviors. Something as simple as changing a flower pot would set Ma Dea off on a tantrum. It took me a while to figure this one out, in spite of the reading I was doing. Sometimes too much knowledge is harmful. I found I could not retain all of the information I was trying to absorb with everything that was going on in my life. Most of the information I learned did not apply to Ma Dea. She was unique and I had to learn how to take one day at a time. I also learned to forgive myself for mistakes and move on.

After that first Christmas fiasco, I made sure Christmas was always exciting in our home. The house was decorated with familiar lights and ornaments and Christmas carols played softly in the background. There were gifts wrapped in colorful paper under the old artificial tree and the house smelled of freshly baked goods and special dishes for Christmas dinner. Ma Dea could not wait until midnight on Christmas Eve so she could wake me to point out her gifts under the Christmas tree. She would open each one carefully and then rewrap it, and put it back under the Christmas tree. Then we would go back to bed and wait for Christmas morning. When the rest of the family arrived, she went through the process of opening her gifts all over again. When she was upset, no one had a happy holiday. Gifts became less important as *My Ladybug's Alzheimer's Journey* progressed. Her happiness became a fleeting target.

It became more and more difficult to find things that would hold Ma Dea's interest for any length of time. She loved to entertain, so in the beginning I planned small social gatherings at our home as often as I could. I tried retiring to my bedroom when my presence agitated her. However, someone always followed and that would upset her. I was trying to honor the commandment she had taught me as a little girl, which is found in Exodus 20:12, "Honour thy father and thy mother: that thy days may be long upon the land which the Lord thy God giveth thee." I failed so many times. If I were to receive a grade on my report card of life, the best I could mark myself would be fair. If only I had been wise enough to see what was really happening with Ma Dea and gotten professional assistance.

I learned through experience that there were times when we both needed our own space. One fall day I came home from work to find that Ma Dea had moved out. The reason was not important; however, when I called the telephone number she had left and found that she was safe; I did not try to persuade her to return home. Apparently she needed to be away for a while. I worried about her, but knew the lady where she had gone was a friend and would take care of her needs.

I prayed that the Lord would give me the patience and knowledge to deal with my mother. I remembered the words of Philippians 4:13, "I can do all things through Christ which strengtheneth me." Not only did I realized that I needed help in understanding the changes in my mother, I needed strength to endure. Proverbs 3:5-6 came to mind, "Trust in the Lord with all thine heart; and lean not unto thine own understanding. In all thy ways acknowledge him, and he shall direct thy paths." I had to learn to trust God for everything, because she looked like my mother, but she did not act like my mother.

Always Mother's Child

My mother's illness taught me to listen with my heart and to respond out of love. Ma Dea saw me as her child and not as an adult. That was a hard pill to swallow. I came to understand that one afternoon when I entertained a small group of close friends at our home.

It was not uncommon for her to join in on conversations. It became obvious to me that Ma Dea did not consider me an equal because I had no children. Whenever I tried to add to the conversation about children, she would tell me to be quiet. I felt frustrated when that happened, but tried not to make an issue out of her unusual behavior.

My friends thought it was funny that Ma Dea treated me like one of the children. They would tease me about it when she left the room, saying jokingly, "*Go and play with the other children.*" I understood that my mother and friends had a common bond in that they had children and age did not matter. When they talked about their children, she talked about me and my brothers. I learned to find humor in small things and not to take unimportant things so seriously.

That was just the surface of the problem. The problem was not restricted to entertaining company. Ma Dea would take over business discussions and make decisions for me as well. There were times when I found out about repairs that needed to be done when the repairman showed up at the door to do the work or when the work had already been completed and payment was required. She made decisions based on the recommendations of her friends. My opinion seemed of no value to her, but ultimately I had to choose the battles I wanted to fight.

In public, Ma Dea appeared to be happy and loving towards me, but at home she was a different person. I tried to get closer to her, but mending our relationship seemed to be impossible. When I tried to talk with her about whatever was bothering her, she would just resort to tears or yelling. Only the family and very close friends knew what was really going on at our home. I am sure she thought I was trying to usurp her authority.

Ma Dea was the matriarch of the family and ruled with an iron fist. The age and statue of her adult children was of no consequence. Her five feet, five frame towered head and shoulder over us in authority. At the time of the onset of the Alzheimer's disease, my older brother stood five feet, eleven, and I am six feet with the baby of the family being six feet, three inches tall, and our ages ranged from forty five to fifty eight, Ma Dea only saw us as her children.

My mother always demanded respect whether reasonable or unreasonable, and she was entitled. My brothers were not accepting that there was anything wrong with Ma Dea and I was not aware of the avenues of help that were available. Besides at that point, my mother would not listen to anyone I recommended. I knew that she would reject interference from an outsider.

Up to the point when Ma Dea was confined to the bed, other people could usually persuade her to do things that were impossible for me to manage. Basically, she saw me as her child not her adult daughter. The depth and breadth of the problems continued to amaze me. One of the things that caught me by surprise was when she asked me to bring my paycheck home and let her manage the money. She wanted to pay the bills and give me an allowance out of the money that was left over. I was speechless to say the least. I should have been grateful that she did not demand that I comply. At least I had the option of refusing although I knew it would lead to trouble. I tried to explain that those arrangements worked for her friends because they were husband and wife not mother and daughter. It took a lot of soul searching on my part before I realized that in a strange way she did not see a difference in our relationship.

A critique of some of my actions suggests that I was still trying to gain Ma Dea's approval at the age of fifty four. In many ways I tried to buy her respect. I did not know it at the time, but I tried to make up for the things she had missed in her life. I paid all household expenses and supplemented her minimal income; provide a car for her to drive and a credit card for gas. I saw to it that she was able to take at least one vacation each year. The things I tried to do for her were never successful. I did not realize that her problem was much deeper than things.

Initially I felt burdened over Ma Dea's reaction to situations in our home. The conditions were very stressful and I prayed for understanding and relief. God always had a way of bringing scriptures to my remembrance for comfort like I Peter 5:6-7, "Therefore humble yourself under the mighty hand of God that He may exhalt you in due time," "Casting all your care upon him; for he careth for you." I finally put the problem in his hands after many failures. Instead of feeling burdened, I was able to put things in the right perspective.

The person I was living with looked like my mother but she was not acting like the mother I had known all my life and I had to learn to accept that. In many ways she was a stranger to me. One of the most devastating things I found was that her moral values had changed. The values she had taught me as a child went out of the window. Ma Dea wanted me to agree to a strange man and his dog living in our basement. I was in shock for days after she mentioned it. I had never met the man and was not sure how she knew him. The request was totally out of character for my mother. My mother had never allowed a man to spend the night in our home when I was growing up. I understood that we were both adults and things were different, but I had a problem with a man and dog staying in the basement of our home and told her that I did not agree.

Ma Dea got very indignant with me when I refused to consider her request to let the man stay in the basement. She screamed, *"Just who do you think you are telling me what to do."* She let me know that she was an adult, and this was her home. I did not respond because I knew it would only infuriate her more. Of course she was right. It was her home, but I knew she would have never made that decision when I was growing up. I kept thinking, she looked like my mother, but she does not act like my mother. I did not give in and our relationship was almost stretched beyond repair. All I could do was pray to God for guidance because I was walking in uncharted territory.

I was perplexed and felt helpless over the multiple changes I was witnessing in my mother. It was unclear what she expected of me from day to day. I felt blessed when we got through a few days without outbursts. When I left for work every day, I was never sure what I would find when I returned home. I felt guilty when Ma Dea was away on vacation because I was relieved. However, it was not unusual for her to call with unrealistic requests. An example is when she called me from her home town and wanted me to purchase a home in that city for her and a new boyfriend. I seemed to be more efficient in dealing with her long distance, no matter how strange the request.

The status of our mother daughter relationship had deteriorated to the point that I was not exactly sure what to think. I felt overwhelmed. Ma Dea made it very clear to all present one day during a family meeting. The meeting was really between her and her siblings and I was not sure why I had been invited. As it turned out, the meeting was called to deal with a financial matter. When I attempted to offer input in the discussion, my mother would ask me to keep quiet. I was about to excuse myself from the meeting when the amount of money each person needed to contribute to the cause was mentioned, I stayed because I knew that Ma Dea had no money. That is when I realized why I had been invited to attend the meeting.

The discussion got very interesting when one uncle indicated that he would not be making a contribution because of his wife's objection. Ma Dea proceeded to explain to him that it was his obligation and questioned whether he was a man or a mouse. You can imagine my surprise when my uncle responded that she was not contributing money but that I was. That was a mistake. My mother politely informed him that what was mine was hers. I sat quietly and listened as they thrashed out the problem, knowing that a response from me would create an unpleasant explosion.

I spent many sleepless nights evaluating and wrestling with what it would take to keep peace and still remain in control of my mother's well being. She was correct in a sense, what was mine did belong to her. It is a tough decision to make when it means giving up your identity in order to survive. It was apparent that Ma Dea could not live alone anymore. She appeared to be normal, but in many ways, her actions spoke volumes to the contrary.

I had come to a point where I could not accept making a change in my mother's living arrangements. I counted up the emotional and financial cost and prayed that I would be able to stand the storm. I came to realize that living under the stress of taking care of Ma Dea and working could lead to physical problem. I talked it over with my doctor and he provided the stability I needed. In some cases he prescribed medication, but I am thankful that I remained relatively healthy through the twelve years and eleven month ordeal.

Medical Problems Intensified

In addition to everything else going on in her life, Ma Dea was plagued by what she called female problems. However, she really did have legitimate medical problems prior to the Alzheimer's diagnosis. She had surgery on her right lung because of tuberculosis. She also had surgery for hemorrhoids, a mastectomy and cataract surgery on both eyes. She was first diagnosed with dementia after having back surgery in March of 1995. Her cognition got significantly worse after the back surgery, and she was never the same after the bypass surgery in December of the same year. I don't think I had ever heard of or paid attention to the term Alzheimer's disease prior to that time.

During the hours I spent taking care of my mother, I had time to reflect on her life's journey. Recalling events in her life reinforced the conclusion that her problem started long before the dementia and Alzheimer's disease diagnosis. She had hidden emotions that surfaced on her Alzheimer's journey that identified how she had learned to cope with the circumstances she had been dealt by life.

There was no way of us knowing how insecure Ma Dea really was until the onset of illness. During the course of the Alzheimer's disease her actions showed without a doubt the importance of her children in her life. It became very clear that we were her reason for living and when we grew up and moved out on our own, she was terrified. The fact that we continued to play major roles in her life did not seem to make a difference.

So, although the book is called *"My Ladybug's Alzheimer's Journey,"* in reality the journey really began long before the diagnosis of Alzheimer's disease. However, the portion of the journey following the diagnosis is what caused my heart to break many times over during the twelve years and eleven months Ladybug struggled with the disease and the devastating impact it had on both of our lives.

Chapter 4
Dementia Emerges Unexpectedly

Back Surgery in 1995

It was after back surgery in the spring of 1995 that I had my first encounter with "dementia", and it terrified me. I had become accustomed to Ma Dea complaining about back aches because it had been going on for a number of years. That is why it caught me by surprise the day she abruptly informed me that she was having back surgery. I needed verification from her doctor, so I persuaded her to let me accompany her to her next appointment. To my dismay, the doctor verified that she needed to have surgery on her back. He went over the procedure and requirements with us, and I agreed to take her to have blood drawn several weeks prior to the scheduled surgery in case she needed blood during or after the surgery. I left the doctor's office concerned because of my mother's age, but the decision was hers to make.

The day of the surgery arrived, and my brothers and I took Ma Dea to the hospital. We prayed for her before they took her up for surgery and prepared for the long wait. We waited; it seemed forever, in the surgical lounge for the operation to be over. The surgeon finally came out to talk with our family. He felt that the procedure had been a success and informed us that she would be in recovery for several hours before we would be allowed to see her for a few minutes.

The Battles Begin

We thought our worries were over after we talked with Ma Dea in the recovery room. So, both brothers left the hospital, and I waited for her to be moved to a semi-private room. I stayed with her as planned to make sure she was settled in her room for her hospital stay. While I sat with her, I noticed that she seemed delirious at times, but I thought it had something to do with the anesthesia used for the surgery. After a couple of hours I had to calm her down to keep her from attacking her roommate for no reason. I was getting afraid because I didn't know what was happening with her emotions. I got permission to stay with her the first night in the hospital, which turned into me staying every night with her during her hospital confinement. My emotions at that point ran from shock to embarrassment and then to disbelief at how my mother was acting. This lady looked like my mother, but she was not acting like my mother.

I never felt more helpless than that first night as I sat with Ma Dea in that hospital room. I repeated the 23rd number of Psalms over and over trying to find comfort. I didn't know how to pray for her because I didn't know what was happening in her life. I just knew that my mother was a stranger. She looked like my mother, but she did not act like my mother. How do you deal with not recognizing your mother whom you love and who have been a father and mother to you for so many years? She could be very difficult at times, but she was still my mother and with the Lord's help I dealt with it. This experience with her was totally new.

The rest of Ma Dea's stay in the hospital was difficult for me, but I am sure it was more difficult for her to understand. I could not imagine what she was thinking. She continued to do things that were totally out of character. I felt a little better after talking with her doctor about her condition. He told me that sometimes older patients were disoriented for four or five days after major surgery but would return to normal. I was relieved to hear the news that she would return to normal. I was looking forward for the nightmare to be over when I took her home.

One unforgettable incident during Ma Dea's hospital stay is when they had to give her blood. To everyone's surprise, the fight was on the moment she saw the blood. When the nurse came into the room with the blood, she grabbed it. The nurse was trying to protect the blood, but they struggled all over the room. I was in shock and could not move. My mother was seventy-two years old and was recovering from back surgery, but she fought the nurse for the blood as if she were a healthy young woman. I had never seen her act that way. When they calmed her down, the room was covered with blood and none was in my mother. I was amazed.

I could not explain the changes that were taking place with Ma Dea while she was in the hospital. My younger brother had to experience it first hand before he understood what was happening. It happened early one morning after I had spent an exhausting night with her, I asked him to come to the hospital and relieve me for a while. When he arrived, he was also shocked at the things she was doing. After I left the room to take a break, he tried to talk with her about her behavior. She got hysterical and became very combative. In typical male fashion, he slapped her face lightly trying to snap her out of the hysteria. She was still talking about how he had hit her when I returned to her room. He was her youngest child and could usually do more with her than anyone else but not this time; she was angry for months after she had been released from the hospital.

The doctor reported that physically Ma Dea was making good progress. After a few days of physical therapy, she was doing well enough to go home. To everyone's surprise, my mother decided she didn't want to go home that day and acted up so badly that I was ashamed of her. She wouldn't do anything the therapist or nurse asked her to do. She was uncooperative and rude to everyone. When the nurse tried to discuss with me how to take care of her when she got home, that was the last straw. She went berserk. I could not believe my eyes. This lady looked like my mother, but she did not act like my mother.

The change that came over Ma Dea's face during an emotional episode that took control of her mind both shocked and frightened me the first time I witnessed it while she was in the hospital. It was as if a curtain had been pulled down just behind the surface. Her features were the same but the blank look showed no emotions. It looked as if she was looking at me and the piercing look went through my body and there was no sign of recognition. I learned to recognize the look and to be prepared for anything. I could not put my finger on what the change was other than the expression on her face, but there was no visible recognition of my mother behind the mask.

Home after Back Surgery in 1995

I still have not figured out why Ma Dea did not want to come home, unless she didn't recognize me as her daughter. They finally gave up on sending her home that day and decided to let her stay in the hospital another day. They really didn't have a choice. They would have had to put her in restraints to get her out of the hospital that day. However, she surprised everyone the following day by agreeing to come home with me without protesting. Little did I know; that was just the beginning of what would be a long battle with a horrible disease.

Everything seemed almost normal at home. Ma Dea recovered from the surgery without any more physical complications; however, her cognitive processes were something less than normal. I stayed home with her the first week and found a lady to stay with her when I went back to work. After a couple of weeks, she was doing well enough to stay home alone, and I was thankful for that. The only problem was that I noticed that she was more forgetful than usual. She was constantly leaving water running and flooding the kitchen and bathroom floors. She managed to set off the burglar alarm and lock herself out of the house or her car several times a week. Her ability to reason was impaired.

My role as her daughter changed drastically. Ma Dea became very dependent and that was the extreme opposite of what life had been like prior to the back surgery. However, I made the adjustment. I got use to being called home from work when she was confused and didn't know what to do about a situation she had created. I tried to reassure her that everything was all right to keep her from worrying. So very quickly I have to move from being the child to being the parent.

It was not unusual for me to receive calls from my burglar alarm provider to report one problem or another. One time my front door had been left open and other times the sensor was turned on while inside doors were left ajar. There were also times when the alarm was going off for no apparent reason. One day the police had been sent out, because I was on the way home and the burglar alarm dispatcher could not reach me. I had just gotten in the house good when I saw a policeman jumping the fence in the backyard. I looked out the window and police surrounded the house. My mother was nowhere to be found. I had to show identification that I actually lived there and was the home owner before they would leave.

Hospital Emergency

One day I received a call from my sister-in-law that my mother had been rushed to the hospital. I was surprised that I had not received a call and wondered how my sister-in-law had found out, but the important thing was that she had received help. When I got to the hospital, they could not understand exactly what the problem was because she was not communicating clearly. I later found out that Ma Dea had called the doctor's office and complained of a headache. To be safe, they sent an ambulance to transport her to the nearest hospital. The hospital happened to be one that she had never been to and her doctor was not on staff. When I shared her medical history with the doctors, they ran tests and found nothing. They released her and I brought her home.

The mystery of why Ma Dea had called the doctor's office was never resolved. However, the lesson learned was that I could not depend on my mother to explain clearly exactly what her medical condition was at any given moment. It was my job to make sure that all her records were updated with the correct contact information. As after thought was that maybe that was my warning that in the very near future, she would not be able to say home alone.

I started to read articles and books on dementia and Alzheimer's disease. I read everything I could get my hands on. I had also found a new doctor who specialized in geriatrics. The surgeon that had performed the back surgery recommended him. I had not been permitted to accompany her to doctor's appointments prior to that time, and was unhappy with some of the medication she was taking prior to the change in doctors, but she was adamant about me not talking with her doctor. Through my reading I found out that Ma Dea did not actually following the norm for Alzheimer's disease. I would have been surprised if she had. Her new doctor assured me that it was not unusual for her condition to deviate.

Fear of the Dark

As time went on, I found out that Ma Dea had developed a fear of the dark. One Sunday evening I came home from church and found her sitting in the living room with a gun she had brought from the South. She told me that someone had climbed up in one of the trees and cut a hole in the roof and came into the house. I went all over the inside and outside of the house to reassure her that there was no hole in the roof and no one was in the house. To comfort her we went over our favorite scriptures, Psalms 23 and 91 and then II Timothy 1:7. I don't think they were of much comfort, but she did calm down after a while. After several episodes of that nature, I made sure someone stayed with her if I could not take her with me on the evenings I went out. There were often times when she did not want to go with me for whatever reason and I had to make other arrangements.

My older brother finally had his first hand experience with Ma Dea's irrational behavior on one evening I had to go out. I left her with him and his young daughter while I attended an event at church. I returned home to find that she had become upset when my brother failed to understand some point she was trying to make. She had tried to take her car keys and leave the house, but he was afraid for her to drive when she was so angry. He took the keys away from her thinking that would prevent her from leaving. Well, that was his mistake. She walked out of the house wearing only a housecoat and a pair of slacks. He was so alarmed that when he finally got his thoughts together to go after her, she was out of sight. He didn't realize how fast she could move.

My niece met me at the door jumping up and down shouting, *"Granny has gone down the street."* At first I thought she was playing a game. Her father assured me that our mother had really left and had not returned. My brother was so distraught, he was near tears. He kept apologizing to me for letting Ma Dea leave the house. He eventually understood when I explained that the behavior was not new to me and that it was what I had tried to explain to him before but was unsuccessful.

After I spent a stressful night trying to find her, she called the following morning and asked me to come and bring her home. When she had left home the night before, she had gone to a neighbor's house, and he took her to the home of a long time friend. She had no idea where she was when she called me. I asked to speak with someone in the house with her, and they were able to give me directions to the house. It was amazing that when she was in that agitated state, Ma Dea could be very coherent but confused when in a calmer state. Her memory just did not function in the same way. She remembered that my brother had taken her car keys but not what the fight was about. She told me he had hit her, and I was sure he would never do that, not even to try and snap her out of becoming hysterical as my younger brother had done in the hospital. I asked her to show me where he had hit her, and she could not. By the time I got her home, she was so frustrated with me that she laid on the floor in her bedroom and cried for hours. My mistake was not agreeing with her report of what had happened.

When I picked Ma Dea up from the friend's home I was dressed for church because I had an appointment to take a group picture. My mother was so distraught I could not get her dressed for church. I called the church to let them know that she was not well and not to wait to include me in the picture. Two of my close friends came over to see if they could help after the picture was taken. When they arrived my mother had decided to get up from the floor and was behaving as if nothing had happened. My friends had lunch with us before returning to church for an afternoon program. To everyone's surprise, when they got up to leave, Ma Dea wanted to accompany them to church. I had no choice but to get her dressed and take her to church to avoid another outburst. When we walked in the church, people kept coming up to me to say they thought my mother was not well. All I could say was that she was feeling better. I had learned not to be ashamed or try to explain her behavior.

Driving Becomes a Problem

The fact that my older brother was concerned enough to take the car keys to prevent my mother from driving reinforced my fears about her driving the car. It was evident that her memory loss and erratic behavior made driving the car a danger to her and other drivers on the road. Normally, she did not like driving at night. However, it was not unusual for her to still be out when I got home from work. This presented a serious problem because my mother was very independent and taking the car away from her was taking away her freedom and she was not going to give it up easily. I was not anxious to begin the struggle I would have to go through to prevent her from driving.

A friend visiting from New York clarified for me why Ma Dea sometimes returned home so late. They went visiting old friends one day while I was at work, and my mother got lost and had to ask a stranger on the street for directions. She still could not find her way and had to stop several more times before she finally arrived at her destination and home again. That propelled the campaign to take away her driving privileges. I tried to persuade her to stop driving, but giving up the car was not something she was willing to discuss. She had lost her car keys so many times I was afraid someone would just get in the car and drive it away. That might have been a good solution to the problem, but it never happened.

Another concern I had with Ma Dea driving the car was that she had always been an outgoing person. She would talk to people on the street, in the supermarket, or in the doctor's office; it did not matter to her. I was afraid that someone would see that she was confused and follow her to the car and take advantage of her and steal the car. I tried numerous ways to convince her not to go out in the car alone any more, but they all ended up with her being hysterical and out of control. All I could do was pray that the Lord would send a guardian angel to watch over her and keep her safe, and he always looked out for her safety.

I got a slight reprieve from forcing the driving issue when my mother became so preoccupied with other things that she forgot about driving the car for a while. But when she grew tired of the new found attraction, her mind became fixated on driving the car again. When she was not permitted to drive, she would get upset and threaten to kill herself in some drastic way. She would get so angry that I was afraid that she would actually go through with her threats. I prayed and asked God to show me how to take care of removing the car out of her reach.

One day while driving with Ma Dea, I came up with what I thought was the perfect answer. Her next doctor's appointment was near, so I would ask the doctor if he would tell her she couldn't drive anymore. I figured she would listen to him. But low and behold, he wanted no part of my plan. Instead he referred me to the Secretary of State and suggested that they test her and prove she could not make decisions well enough to drive. I really couldn't blame him for not wanting to upset her.

Then I remembered that she had really acted up in his office one day when her friend had taken her to the doctor. His nurse had experienced my mother at her worst. Her regular doctor was out of the office and one of his colleagues saw her that day. She was so possessed with driving, she asked him if she could drive and he responded in the negative. She performed so in the doctor's office they had to give her Prozac to calm her. When I arrived home and noticed her strange behavior, I threw the medication away because I decided it was better to have her the way she was than have her under the influence of the medication.

After many tantrums and episodes, with the help of God, I resolved the issue of my mother driving the car. I had my younger brother come and drive the car over to his house and give it to his son one evening when Ma Dea was asleep. I thought if it were out of sight, she would eventually forget it existed. Well, giving her car away did not deceive her and she told everyone who would listen how I gave it away. She even knew to whom I had given the car. It was a struggle, but eventually she did forget about the car, or she lost the ability to express her displeasure at having her car taken away.

Red Flags of Memory Loss

It came to my attention that Ma Dea's cognition improvements had ended. She was not going to get any better than she was at that moment. I thought she had resumed most of her previous activities without complications when I discovered that her improvements only went to a point and stopped.

I began to notice that familiar things like cooking were becoming more and more of a challenge for Ma Dea. Over the years she had developed into an excellent cook. She could cook almost any dish without following a recipe. One of her favorite desserts was a punchbowl cake. Her friends at church loved her punchbowl cakes. I came downstairs one day to find her wandering around in the kitchen looking frustrated. I asked her what was wrong, and she said, "*I forgot what to put in the cake.*" She had sent me to the store to purchase the ingredients but thought they were the wrong ones. I could not help her because she had never shared the recipe with me.

My mother had also been good at making flowers, pillows and other crafts, but her favorite was sewing. She had been sewing since childhood. She learned to sew by hand because the family where she grew up did not have a sewing machine. She could make fancy stitches by hand that impressed people. She recalled getting punished for cutting up bed sheets to make doll clothes. She took pride in making all of my clothes when I was growing up and even did sewing for friends.

Ma Dea had tried to make a suit for me as she had done many times in the past. It was obvious that she had lost some of her sewing skills. She purchased a pattern and material to make the suit, but it took forever for her to complete the project. Every time she had me try it on there would be something wrong with it. She never got it right but I wore it to please her because she had worked so hard on it. Later during her illness, I found pieces of the material where she had gone out secretly and purchased new material over and over again because she had made mistakes in cutting or sewing the pieces together. It was sad to see her precious skills decline.

It was at this point that I really took a very close look at my mother. She was never going to be the family matriarch again. However, she never gave up trying. Where she had learned to be the decision maker of the family, she was now afraid to make a decision. She suffered from confusion and insecurities. She had become dependent on me for everything. There were times when I saw glimpse of my mother as she had been but not often. She looked like my mother, but she did not act like my mother. She was no longer the controlling figure in my life. That is when she became my Ladybug.

I prayed for an understanding of her problem. I did not feel capable of taking on the total responsibility for her life. Once again God brought to my memory scriptures on which I could depend. One of my favorites that I hold dear is Proverbs 3:5-6, "Trust in the Lord with all thine heart; and lean not unto thine own understanding. In all thy ways acknowledge him, and he shall direct thy paths". This became my companion scripture while on *My Ladybug's Alzheimer's Journey.*

I know that it was not the back surgery that brought on the dementia, but if I had to do it over again, I would try and persuade her not to have that surgery on her back. Maybe it would have deferred the full impact of the disease. I am now of the opinion that surgery should not be performed on senior citizens unless it is life threatening.

Chapter 5
More Serious Illness

Triple Bypass Surgery

In December of that same year, 1995, I had stayed home from work on a personal day. I noticed that Ladybug had left throw rugs on the floor of the Florida room for several days and it was not like her to do that. I was afraid to upset her, but I asked why they were left there. She indicated that she was taking them to the Laundromat, but every time she attempted to take them, she would get so short of breath she couldn't manage to carry them. I called her doctor and told him what was happening, and he instructed me to take her to the hospital Emergency Room.

After examining her, the Emergency Room physician moved Ladybug to the cardiac care unit. To my surprise, there was a problem with her heart. After many tests, the diagnosis was that she had three blocked arteries and needed triple bypass surgery. Her condition was critical, and she was to be hospitalized immediately. I stayed with her through the admission process. I shared my concern about Ladybug's confusion and wandering with the nurse. She assured me that the monitors she had been hooked up to would alert them of every movement she made.

The first thing I did after that was call my brothers. I could not reach my older brother, but my younger brother and his wife joined me at the hospital right away. Arrangements were made for the surgeon to explain what the diagnosis meant and what they planned to do to correct the problem. He wanted to perform the surgery before Christmas, because he would be going out of town for the holidays. Since Christmas was only a week away, the surgery was scheduled for the following day.

When we all got together to talk about what was wrong with our mother, we were sick with fear. It had been less than nine months since the back surgery. The experience of that surgery was still fresh in our memories. We went back to see my mother and prayed with her before leaving the hospital until the next morning when the surgery would be performed. The nurse gave us the telephone numbers and said one of us could call throughout the night to check on her. We got very little sleep that night; I was frozen with fear. I called the hospital to check on my mother every two hours and informed my brothers of her condition.

Compared to the dementia after the back surgery, what was ahead was ten times worse. I was not prepared to cope with the journey ahead of me. We were already terrified for two reasons. First, the mere fact that Ladybug was having surgery on her heart terrified us. Secondly, we remembered what happened after the back surgery. Here we were a few days before Christmas waiting in the Cardiac Surgical Lounge. My older brother was so nervous; he decided to leave the hospital. I was to call him when the surgery was over. Waiting in the surgical lounge that day was almost unbearable. An evangelist from the church came to pray and wait with us for the surgeon's report. As usual, it seemed to take forever before the surgeon called for our family.

The surgery was finally over and the surgeon reported that everything had gone well. We were told to watch for the medical team that would soon be taking Ladybug to the Cardiac ICU Recovery Unit around the corner from the surgical lounge. We anxiously watched as the team rushed by with Ladybug's small body clad in white. It was the most beautiful sight to see her face. The nurse came out after a while to talk with us after Ladybug was settled. She told us that it would be a while before we could visit with our mother, and we were given a schedule of the visiting periods. We understood that it would take longer for Ladybug to become alert, and we waited.

I called my older brother to let him know that the surgery was over and that we were waiting for an opportunity to see her. He made it back to the hospital before we were permitted to go in to visit with our mother. During the first visit, she appeared to be doing well. She knew who we were and even called us by name. The number of tubes and lines protruding from her body shook us, but we breathed sighs of relief and thanked God that the confusion seemed to be absent.

We waited in the surgical lounge for the five minute visits every hour until late in the evening. We shared memories of our childhoods and our lives with our mother. She had been both father and mother to us for a great part of our lives. We were grateful that her life had been spared and that she would be with us a while longer.

After the first day, my brothers went on with their lives and visited once or twice a day. I took up my daily post with Bible in hands and prayers on my lips waiting between visits when I could go in and spend the few allotted minutes with her. The nurses were encouraging and politely answered all of my questions. My mother was kept so sedated that she was not saying much, but I was encouraged. I knew she needed her rest to mend. I was just thankful that she seemed to be making progress.

Ladybug had made enough improvement to be moved to the Cardiac Care Step-Down Unit the last work day before the holidays. I will never forget that day. It was the day of the Christmas celebration at my job. The nurse assured me that it would be all right if I left for a while because she wasn't sure of the exact time they would move Ladybug. So, I left to take Christmas gifts I had previously purchased for employees at work. I stayed and visited with my co-workers for a while after having refreshments and exchanging gifts, but my mind was on Ladybug in the hospital.

Dreaded Confusion Returns

I was anxious when I returned to the hospital. I asked for directions to where they had moved Ladybug, and the nurse just said, *"There she is over there."* My heart dropped to my toes. Ladybug was sitting next to the bed taking the restraints off her wrists. She had already pulled all of the IVs out of her arms. As I approached her I recognized the dreaded blank look on her face that

I had learned to fear. Regrettably, I saw it many more times before the end of her life. I rushed to the telephone to call my brothers but could not reach them. I asked a close friend to keep calling until she was able to make contact with them. I canceled a Christmas gathering I had planned at my home for an out of town friend. Then, I went back to sit by my mother's bedside.

The purpose of moving Ladybug to the Step-Down Unit was to continue her recovery after the heart surgery, but it was very clear her cognition was severely damaged. She never knew that she was even in the hospital; much less had had heart surgery. It was affirmed one night as I sat next to her bed and she asked, *"Are they washing dishes in the kitchen?"* That is when it occurred to me that she didn't have a clue where she was and why she was there. The distress I was feeling was overwhelming. I felt like the weight of the world was on my shoulders. All I could do was pray and stay by her bedside. I left her only to shower and change clothes.

A family member and a sitter stayed at Ladybug's bedside during her entire hospital confinement. The experience was beyond belief. Ladybug's arms and legs were restrained but a sitter was required to be with her at all times. We still couldn't always contain her. Sometimes she managed to get out of the restraints. Can anyone picture a seventy-three year old woman weighing no more than 140 pound, who had just had triple bypass heart surgery, being uncontainable? The strength of that little lady was unbelievable. It took four people to get her back in bed one day after she had managed to escape from the restraints. One of the staff members looked at me surprisingly and asked, *"How old did you say she is?"* The sad thing about the whole experience was that she didn't understand that she was being helped. She just thought she was someplace being held against her wishes.

During her stay in the hospital, Ladybug had adverse reactions to all of the medication they gave her to help with her recovery from the heart surgery and to keep her calm. The only medication they could give her without making her more hyper was Tylenol. Apparently she was never in pain or did not know when she was in pain after the surgery. She was so active she had to be watched every minute. We didn't dare take your eyes off of her or fall asleep. Most of the time, she wasn't saying anything, she was just very busy.

I did not want anyone outside of the family to see how confused Ladybug was. I even called the church and asked the members not to visit her. I just couldn't bear for anyone to see her like that. My emotions were on edge. I was exhausted but afraid to leave her bedside. I could not get over the shock of how much worse she was mentally. I was so depressed I felt like I was in the world all alone. I could not read the Bible; I just prayed that the Lord would take care of my mother and give me the strength to help her. The fact that she was frightened and angry in addition to being confused did not help. She tried to run away every chance she got.

The Sunday before Christmas, I left her bedside to attend the Christmas program at church. As I approached the building, I met a minister and my heart was so heavy I stopped to ask for prayer for my mother. However, the minister had problems of her own. That is when the Lord called to my remembrance I Peter 5:6-7, "Humble yourselves therefore under the mighty hand of God, that he may exalt you in due time: Casting all your care upon him; for he cares for you." At that point I realized man could not help me. Only God could carry the burden I was trying to carry alone. I silently asked the Lord again to take care of my mother and me during this trying period.

Once again we thought Ladybug's recovery had turned the corner after surgery. It was on Christmas Day when I picked up my brothers, and we returned to the hospital to celebrate Christmas with our mother. The sitter got Ladybug out of bed and took us to a sitting area where we could visit with her and open gifts without disturbing her roommate. She remembered all of our names and introduced us to the sitter. We were amazed that she was able to introduce us to anyone. I was so encouraged that I took her into the bathroom and changed her into a new gown, robe and house slippers. We were all encouraged and thankful when we left her at the hospital that Christmas day.

For the first time since the surgery, I felt comfortable leaving the hospital to go home and get some sleep. I thanked God for answering my prayer requests. My sister-in-law had prepared Christmas dinner, and I told her I would be over after I showered, changed clothes and got some rest. Well, the relieved feeling didn't last long. I was awakened by the telephone. The sitter had dialed the number for Ladybug. I heard this small voice saying, "Come *and get me; she hit me*." Of course I jumped up, got dressed and rushed back to the hospital. When I got to the hospital, the sitter swore that she had not hit my mother, but in my heart I knew that she probably did. I don't remember eating Christmas dinner that year.

I realized that my mother was a handful to take care of and that she would do things that would provoke people, but I was also equally sure that she did not mean to hurt anyone. I also knew that she would fight, because she had hit me several times during her illness. Untrained people would probably respond by hitting back. However, I thought it very unprofessional for anyone to hit a sick person. I found Ladybug's nice new Christmas gifts crumpled up in a bag. She had tried to run away, and the sitter said all she could catch was the tail of her robe. She took it off and kept running. She, in fact ran, out of all her clothes. They finally caught her, dressed her in a hospital gown and put her back in bed. I don't have words to express how I felt at that news. I was devastated and disappointed that the perceived improvement in her condition was not true.

I spoke with the nurse about Ladybug's condition, and she had no answers. She informed me that the doctors would be making rounds at 7:00 o'clock the next morning. I told her that I would be there to meet with the doctors. When my mother finally quieted down that Christmas night, I went home to make preparations for bringing her home the next day. I was back at the hospital when the doctors made their rounds the following morning. I talked with the surgeon, and he reinforced what I had been told previously that sometimes patients in Ladybug's condition get better in familiar surroundings.

I asked his permission to take Ladybug home. Other than being confused, physically she seemed to be doing fine. He reiterated that the only medication they had been able to give her that did not make her more confused was Tylenol. So he wrote discharge orders and prescriptions for medication and vitamins and left them with the nurse to process.

The nurses were in disbelief at the news of my taking Ladybug home. One of them asked if I were sure I wanted to take her home? She thought maybe a short term care facility would be a better solution. I responded, *"No, I am taking her home." "If it doesn't work, then I will look for another solution."* The staff rushed around making sure I had everything they thought I would need. In a last minute effort to help, they had a social worker come and talk with me, but my decision was firm.

Ladybug's things were packed and we were finally ready to leave the hospital. I was loaded with telephone numbers and contacts in case I had questions or needed help at home. After I had taken care of everything, and we were thanking the staff for all of their help, one of the nurses wished me luck and said that she was glad I was taking my mother home. She shared with me her worst nightmare. It was seeing my mother on the 6:00 O'clock news, with the caption *"Cardiac Patient Running down the Street."* Then fear hit me and I realized how serious taking Ladybug home could get, but it was too late. Things were already in motion to make it happen and I would not change the process that was taking place. Then, I was encouraged by Philippians 4:13, "I can do all things through Christ which strengtheneth me."

Big Surprise

In reality, Ladybug doing better in familiar surroundings turned out not to be accurate. Maybe it would have been accurate if I could have figured out what surroundings were familiar. It had never occurred to me that she might not recognize her home or me for that matter. I still am not exactly sure when her ability to recognize her children was lost. But I am getting ahead of myself.

On December 26, 1995, the day after Christmas, we were on our way home. We had an unexpected passenger because one of the senior citizens from our church had somehow gotten up to see Ladybug early that morning, even before visiting hours. He came by bus, so I dropped him off at home. My mother didn't recognize him or any of her surroundings as we drove home. I was petrified. I needed to stop by the pharmacy to get her prescriptions filled, but I couldn't leave her in the car in her condition. I didn't want to take her in with me, so I decided to get her home first and have someone get the prescriptions filled later.

I managed to get Ladybug and her things in the house without complications. The blank expression on her face told me she had no memory of ever living in this house. She gazed out the window at the houses and cars in the neighborhood in amazement. I am not sure where she was mentally at that point. I asked if she wanted to put her things in her room, and she looked at me and asked in surprise, *"Do I live here?"* It broke my heart to see that she did not remember her home. We proceeded to her bedroom, and she looked around and commented that it was pretty. To my surprise, she let me put her to bed in this strange room without any fanfare.

My mother woke after taking a brief nap and noticed for the first time the scar on her leg and wanted to know, "*What happened to my leg?*" It was the first of many times I had to explain that she'd had heart surgery and that a vein had been removed from her leg to put in her heart. The first time she saw the scar in her chest it also frightened her, and again she asked the same question, "*What happened to me?*" The routine became very familiar and was repeated many times night and day. Ladybug did not understand the explanations nor could she retain them. The nurse had told me to make sure she was told the same thing every time she asked.

Even though the nurse was scheduled to visit three times a week, I was already questioning my decision to bring Ladybug home. I had no experience in taking care of anyone in her condition. The decision was made with my heart and not my head. I knew that I loved her and would do all within my power to see that she was well cared for, but that gave me little piece of mind. I felt totally inadequate to deal with my mother's special needs. My constant prayer was "*Lord Help me to do the right thing.*" Again, God spoke to me through my companion scriptures found in Proverbs 3:5-6, "Trust in the Lord with all thine heart; and lean not unto thine own understanding. In all thy ways acknowledge him, and he shall direct thy paths."

Immediate Needs Met

In making the decision to bring Ladybug home, I had not taken some key issues into consideration. They were what she would eat, how I would shop for groceries and who would stay with her while I worked. Another thing that frightened me more than anything else was what I would do if she became ill in the middle of the night. The nurse was able to take care of the contact in the middle of the night. She told me I could call her any time. However, I had to figure out the rest.

God came to my rescue once again and sent one of His guardian angels from church to visit Ladybug. It had to be the Lord, because no one knew she was coming home that day. However, the friend volunteered to sit with Ladybug while I shopped for groceries. I returned from the market to find Ladybug angry with the friend. I am not sure what happened, but apparently the lady was also upset. She never came back to see her again. I thanked the lady before she left but she did not explain what had happened during my absence. I prepared my mother favorite foods and prayed that her appetite would be better than it had been during her hospital stay. She ate as if she were starving. "Praise the Lord."

Chapter 6
Many Faces of Alzheimer

Caregivers for Ladybug

I stayed home with Ladybug the first two weeks after she was released from the hospital to make sure her schedule for home health care was in place. After that, a member of my mother's Sunday School class volunteered to stay with her for two weeks to give me time to find a permanent caregiver. I held my breath the first day she came to stay with my mother. But there was no need for worry; God had already worked it out. Ladybug accepted her without comments.

That Sunday while I was taking care of my mother, the Lord placed it on my heart to ask a young woman Ladybug had known since childhood to be her caregiver. She was off work on disability, but she had a medical background that I thought might be helpful. She accepted and we agreed on a small stipend. She was a God send. She was good with my mother.

I am not sure, but I think Ladybug may have remembered the caregiver's mother who was also a church friend. On the surface, that arrangement worked for a while. Only I knew that my mother accused her of stealing her keys and money among other things. However after a while, the caregiver had to resign because of her own physical disabilities. Ladybug's constant involvement in one activity after another was a challenge for the caregiver to deal with.

Ladybug continued to make great strides in her cognition, and her progress was making it very difficult for me to keep caregivers. She really did not want anyone to stay with her and made it known. Her behavior made it very difficult for the caregivers. I finally agreed to let her stay home alone, and I monitored her by telephone to see how it was working. I called throughout the day to make sure she was in the house. By the grace of God, I only had to make trips home occasionally. Family, friends and neighbors had been alerted and they were helpful with watching out for Ladybug while I was at work.

Independent Again

Although my mother was doing well home alone, I worried about her so much that after a couple of months under the stress, I came down with hives around my waist. I made a doctor's appointment for a diagnosis and treatment. He diagnosed it as shingles and said that it probably came from stress. He advised me that it was contagious, and I could not be around pregnant women. Therefore, I could not work until it cleared. It made the next couple of weeks very interesting. It was a blessing in disguise because it gave me an opportunity to observe firsthand how Ladybug functioned without constant supervision. I found that she was able to do quite well on her own. It took twice as long for me to get over the shingles, because I concentrated so hard on my mother's activities. However, I was reassured of her safety while she was on her own.

After being with Ladybug continuously for the two weeks I was encouraged, but I knew that the time would inevitably come when she could not be left alone. Again I thanked God for family and the many friends that helped me take care of emergency situations when I went back to work. When family members had other obligations and could not help, I could always depend on God to send help when I needed it most.

Rehabilitation

Ladybug was doing well enough to attend rehabilitation sessions for her heart. The doctor scheduled her to go to the hospital once a week for the sessions, but I had to make arrangements for transportation. I took her to the first session myself to make sure that it would work for her. I was surprised, but she was all right and seemed to enjoy the interaction with the other patients. My helper, Jesus Christ, dispatched another guardian angel friend to take her to rehabilitation each week without charge. All seemed to be going well until one day when I received a call at work from the friend. He had taken my mother to rehab, but she came right back out and told him she was not staying. I am not sure what she told the therapist, but she refused to stay for the rehab session. When I got home I tried to convince her to return the following week, but she would not reconsider. When she made up her mind not to do something, it was almost impossible to get her to change it.

I called her doctor for advice, but he thought it best not to upset Ladybug by forcing her to return since her resistance was so strong. I never figured out what happened during rehabilitation because the friend always waited for her in the waiting room and was not allowed in the rehab room with her. I could not persuade her to talk about the sessions. There did not appear to be anything physically wrong with Ladybug because she could move around faster than I could when we went out in the evenings and on weekends

The doctor sent Ladybug to a different type of rehabilitation center later on during her journey. He thought it would give her something to occupy part of her time. She was scheduled to attend once a week, and the time was broken up into three different sessions. She would spend thirty-five minutes each with an occupational therapist, a speech therapist and a physical therapist. Ladybug resisted the sessions from day one. As always, I took her for the first series of treatments to make sure she would be all right with them. Then I made arrangements for my sister-in-law to take her for the next sessions.

My sis-in-law had an appointment, and we thought it would be all right for her to leave Ladybug in the care of the therapists until she returned. My mother made it through the session with the occupational therapist and was handed over to the speech therapist for the second thirty five minutes. When my sister-in-law returned, she found my mother sitting on a bench in the hall sobbing. She had been so combative with the speech therapist that she could not do anything with her and had to ask for assistance. My sister-in-law was so concerned, she called me at work. I told her to just take Ladybug home and I would meet them there in an hour.

In an effort to determine what had happened, I took off from work the following week to take Ladybug for her next rehabilitation sessions myself. I sat with her through the occupational therapy session, while she protested. I made it to the speech therapist, but she insisted that I sit in the hall and wait for her. I complied to keep her from becoming irate. When the session was over, the speech therapist came out to see me. She said she had to see what I looked like because from my mother's description, she thought I had horns and a tail. It seems she had spent thirty out of the thirty-five minutes complaining about me. The therapist said she thought she could help her, but she was so angry she could not concentrate. I decided not to try the physical therapy session; I just brought her back home.

Later that year when the family was sitting around after Thanksgiving dinner, we found out what had happened at the rehabilitation session when Ladybug was in tears. She appeared to be talking to herself, but we understood clearly what she was talking about. Apparently she had become combative with the speech therapist when she tried to force her to do something, and when another person came to assist her, it was a real challenge for them to restrain my mother since she was out of control. She said, "*I wrestled those two ladies down on the floor and I was holding them.*" My younger brother was very upset with her about her behavior and tried to reason with her. He asked her if she thought that was the proper way for her to conduct herself. When she didn't respond, it was clear that she knew exactly what she was doing, but she was beyond reasoning. Unfortunately, her days were reduced to staying in the house all day until I could come up with something else for her to do.

Turning Point

It was very difficult to cover all bases where Ladybug was concerned. I experienced a serious wakeup call one day. She found a way to get to the bank, withdraw money and make it to a friend's beauty shop with a fist full of money. The friend was concerned, because she saw her get out of the car with some young men. Only God saved her from being hurt or mugged. How she got to the bank and why she needed money remains a mystery today. The fact that she went to the beauty shop may have meant she wanted to get her hair curled. I am not sure since she did not usually get her hair fixed at that shop. Ladybug loved her children first and money second. It was not like her to give her money to anyone. She was always such a miser. She would not give me money. However, I was thankful that she was all right and that my friend called to let me know what had happened.

The bank incident made me realize that I could not put off applying for guardianship over my mother for her protection. I had delayed it because she had always been so independent and I was afraid it would be a major blowup when I mentioned it to her. I met with my brothers and they agreed that it was time and that I should be the one to petition the probate court for guardianship. My mother would have never agreed to that under normal conditions. Thankfully, when the time came she agreed. Whether or not she knew what she was agreeing to, I am not sure. The first step after filing the papers was to go before the probate judge. I took her with me praying all the way that she would not get aggressive. God was in the plan, and the judge did not even ask her any questions.

The next step was for a court appointed officer to come out and do an in home investigation. When the officer from the court came Ladybug smiled a lot and sat very quietly without raising any objections. I could tell she did not understand what was happening, but she was in a good mood so everything went smoothly. He made a favorable recommendation and the guardianship was approved. I felt better equipped to make decisions that were best for Ladybug in the instances where she was out of control and outside intervention was necessary.

Then I took her to the bank along with the paperwork and had my name put on her account. She signed where she was told to sign without any problem. I had to make sure she could not take money out of the bank without me being with her. Thankfully she was still at the stage where she would do what I asked her to do some of the time. The bank manager knew my mother and the family, so she was very helpful in putting instructions on the account to prevent her from putting herself in danger by taking money out of the account when she was alone. To be safe, after the bank episode, I always made sure she had a couple of dollars in her pocket.

Confused Speech

The first signs of Ladybug's sinking deeper into Alzheimer's disease came several years later. It was when she started to lose the ability to complete sentences and then the ability to speak syllables clearly. Although it appeared to happen suddenly, I am sure it had been happening over a period of time. It was becoming more and more difficult for her to find the right words to get her thoughts across. When I spoke with her doctor about it; he indicated that in most cases the communications skills did not dissipate so quickly. However, there were variances in Alzheimer patients. The fact that my mother was having problems expressing herself aggravated her, and she became very aggressive.

I continued to read information on Alzheimer's disease looking for pitfalls to avoid. The doctor had given me medication that would make Ladybug sleep when she was frustrated. It knocked her out for four hours at a time. I didn't like that; because where-ever it took effect is where she had to stay until it wore off. So I only gave it to her in extreme situations. However, I knew it was time to hire a permanent caregiver for Ladybug. I had no other choice. Her inability to communicate with me by telephone took away the option of her staying home alone. The possibility of her leaving the house and not being able to tell anyone where she belonged was a major concern.

I interviewed several people to take care of Ladybug without success. Once again the Lord intervened and sent a former church member to the rescue. I was comfortable with the person she recommended to serve as caregiver for Ladybug. She agreed to stay with my mother the eight hours I was at work plus the travel time. The drawback was that she did not have transportation and that presented a problem. It created a hardship for me, because I had to pick her up every morning and take her home in the evenings. Even though it added to my day, I think it was harder on Ladybug, because I had to get her up and dressed to take her with me every morning at the time she was just falling asleep.

Ladybug's cognition problems had returned in full force and the medication the doctor gave her did not seem to be helping. Her doctor explained that even at the initial onset of the disease, she was too far along in the progression for the medicine that was currently available to be effective. He reinforced what I had read about Alzheimer's disease. With my limited knowledge, I understood that all Alzheimer's disease patients did not always follow the same progression steps identified in the literature I had read. I found no comfort in knowing that there were no cure for her sickness and there were no way to watch out or prepare for her actions.

Constant Motion

Evenings and weekends were exciting for both of us because I was with Ladybug from Friday evening until Monday morning without a break. She did not sleep very much at night. The doctor called it "Sundowners Syndrome." She was usually quiet and took naps during the day, but she was always very busy after sundown. Her favorite thing to do was to take all of her clothes out of her drawers and closets and pile them near a door, sometimes the front door, sometimes the back door. She would also move pots and pans from the kitchen cabinets and pieces of furniture from all over the house. She would not be satisfied until she had everything near the door. I would try to distract her, but I had very little success most of the time. She was preparing to move.

It was amazing that no matter what activity Ladybug was engaged in, she always had reverence and respect for God. When I grew weary, I would use several techniques to slow her down for a while. One way was to pray, and the other way was to read the Bible. For example, I remember one evening when she had been extremely active; she was on her way across the bed for some unknown reason. I asked her to stop and pray with me. She stopped long enough for me to pray, but when I said *"Amen"*, she was off again. I don't know what I would have done without the Lord. The 23rd Psalms and prayer became my constant companions.

Ladybug would usually settle down at daybreak. But unfortunately during the week it was time for me to get ready for work. I searched my memory for a reason for the constant moving. I recalled that when we were children, we moved a lot. Some people did not rent to people with children especially for the money my mother could afford to pay. Consequently, she was always looking for someplace better for us to live. When she found a place, we would move. Knowing why Ladybug was always moving did not keep me from being exhausted all the time. At least I understood and found peace with the activity. During those times I found John 16:33, to be helpful because it was that peace that I found in Jesus that helped me make it through those nights.

I had already had deadbolt locks put on all entrance and exit doors to prevent Ladybug from leaving the house. Having locks put on the internal doors was the next step. The locks kept Ladybug from moving her clothes from place to place. However, that only cut down on that particular activity; she found other things to replace the ones that had been taken away.

I found Ladybug to be extremely clever during her struggles with Alzheimer's disease. She still had the cooking utensils and a whole house full of furniture to move. I watched her move the dining room table that seats six people late one night. I was at a loss for what to do. I was exhausted from replacing furniture and objects before my days began. One day I was so tired I could not concentrate on my work. When I went to lunch, I fell asleep at the table. I called a friend who was home on Fridays and asked if I could come to her house and sleep until five o'clock. I could not face the weekend without rest. I thank God for the friends he sent to help me.

Silent and Combative

I was becoming more concerned about Ladybug because I noticed that she was becoming more withdrawn when I was with her for long periods of time. Even though she was having problems expressing herself, previously she was always chattering about something. I thought the reason she was not responding to me was because she didn't understand when I tried to engage her in conversation. However, I discovered by talking with the various caregivers that she was trying to communicate with them. It was much later that I learned that she really had a problem with just who I was at times. She was probably trying to figure out why a stranger was trying to take over her life.

Not knowing why Ladybug had become silent while alone with me, I tried harder to get her involved in things on weekends and in the evening when we were alone. I took her out for breakfast on Saturday mornings, because she had always enjoyed eating out. At first she responded positively to that, but she soon grew tired after a while and it was difficult to keep her focused. My goal was to keep her involved in familiar routines that she had enjoyed in the past. We would go to church on Sundays and sometimes during the week for special services. It was not easy to keep her entertained. Even though I was not getting an indication of how she was feeling, I could not give up.

While on *My Ladybug's Alzheimer's Journey*, she insisted on trying to maintain her independence. I learned from literature I was reading that often times the person closest to a sick person is the one who becomes the object of his or her anger and frustrations. Knowing Ladybug, I could understand her resentment at my interference in her life. I even understood that the temper tantrums were her way of expressing her unhappiness. I was just at a loss as to what to do to correct the situation. She looked like my mother, but she did not act like my mother. My prayer before taking her away from the house was that the Lord would guide me in doing the things that would keep her calm and keep us both safe.

Ladybug continued to amaze me by expressing herself clearly when she was angry. She would call people on the telephone and try to tell them that I was doing things that were not true. I knew that it was the illness that made her say hurtful things. I found peace knowing that she loved me and was not aware of what she was doing. What concerned me more was that she was not in control. I also knew that she looked like my mother, but that she did not act like my mother. I prayed for more understanding when people told me the things she was saying, but I knew in my heart that what I was doing was for her good and protection.

I eventually came to a point where I found comfort in knowing that people who knew me also, knew that I was not doing the things Ladybug was saying. I was too busy trying to take care of my mother to worry about what she was saying. My life was so stressed at the time; I did not have the time or the energy to worry about the people who believed what she was saying.

Adult Protective Services

Things got so bad that Ladybug complained to someone, and they gave her the telephone number for Adult Protective Services. I don't think she knew what the number was or what she was doing when she called the number. I am not even sure she made the call. I could not believe that my mother would knowingly do that to me, her daughter. I found the number in her Bible only a few days before I received a letter from Adult Protective Services. I had heard my mother say that God does not let anything slip up on people that trust in Him, and now I believed her proverb. I asked her who had given her the number, but she either did not understand me or did not care to answer. I could not identify the number, so I dialed it to see who would answer. The person on the other end was very rude and would only say that someone would be out to investigate. I thanked God for the warning.

I prayed that if Ladybug wanted to be separated from me that God would remove the desire. I dreaded the visit from the Adult Protective Services Investigator; although, I was confident that my mother was being taken care of very well. I was not concerned about her living conditions, but I was concerned about the unexpected. After praying about it, I had faith that the issue would be resolved in my mother's favor. I knew staying with me was best. So, on the day of the appointment, armed with faith, I took off from work to meet with the investigator. After the lady interviewed me and inspected my mother's living conditions, she saw that Ladybug was clean and appeared to have had an adequate amount of food to eat. All of her needs had been taken care of as well, and she indicated that she found no reason to keep the case open. I thanked God for another answered prayer.

Chapter 7
Connections with the Past

Ladybug was not accepting me, in reality, she seemed to ignore me and I didn't know how to repair that condition. I thought a change in scenery might bring about a change in her disposition. Her only surviving brother was in the hospital in Florida. Visiting him was something Ladybug would have wanted to do under normal circumstances. I planned a trip south with Florida being the first stop and then my mother's home town and surrounding towns. I hoped that going back home might improve her cognition. She had always looked forward to going home on vacations in the past. I was hoping this would be just what the doctor ordered.

I made several mistakes in planning the trip. Mistake number one was I initially planned to travel by plane. However, it became very clear that Ladybug was afraid to fly. She protested violently when I told her that we were going on the plane; I immediately change our mode of transportation. My reason for entertaining the idea of flying was that it would be faster and Ladybug would not get as restless and agitated. Then, I would rent a car for the shorter trips. Her fear of flying was something new because she had flown many times in her lifetime. Looking back over the trip, maybe that is when I should have canceled the trip. But I still thought it was a good idea to take her back to the place she called home.

I changed our mode of transportation to traveling by car. I prayed for protection and traveling grace for our travels. Then I had the car serviced, packed our bags, and drove south on Interstate 75. I realized my second mistake before we reached the Michigan and Ohio borders. I should have invited someone to accompany us to help distract Ladybug and keep her occupied as I drove. A companion was not needed in Plan A, but definitely a requirement for Plan B, travel by car.

Traveling Attitude

My efforts to engage Ladybug in conversation as we traveled failed. Pointing out the beautiful scenery was usually her favorite topic to talk about, but not on this trip. I tried pointing out the Mall Outlet near Flat Rock, Michigan because I had taken her there before and thought she might remember, but she showed no interest. Ladybug always liked listening to Christian music on the radio when we traveled, but she did not pay much attention to the music this time. My last resort was playing simple games that had always worked in the past. I tried being creative and saying the alphabets and numbers backwards. It never occurred to me to just say them in their normal order. I should have realized that saying them out of the normal order confused and frustrated her.

My efforts to entertain Ladybug only caused her to be more depressed. She was not a happy traveler. Going through the mountains in Kentucky and Tennessee were usually high points when we traveled by car. However, on this trip she found no fascination in seeing the small towns and communities tucked between the mountains and hillsides. She just sat quietly in her seat without any type of expression and only spoke to ask, *"Are you tired?"* or *"Are you sleepy?"* every few miles. I had no idea what she was thinking and that worried me. As an afterthought, I realized that driving probably was not a good idea either. I think that maybe Ladybug was afraid. I said to myself, *"You must have neglected to ask God to direct your paths or misinterpreted His answer before starting out on the trip."*

My mother had always loved eating at different restaurants when we traveled by car, so I prayerfully stopped often. This made our progress very slow. My worst fear was that she would become upset, and I would not be able to control her in the restaurants. I tried not to upset her by letting her decide where to eat and how long we would stay. As a result, we arrived at our hotel in Atlanta Georgia four hours later than projected. I thanked God that I had made reservations at the midway point, so we would not have a problem finding a place to rest for the night.

Unexpected Fear

Both Ladybug and I were exhausted when we arrived at the hotel. I ordered something light to eat in the room just in case she was hungry. Going out to eat was not an option because of her mood. Eating was not a priority for her anyway because we had stopped to eat often. I soon discovered that she was afraid of the unfamiliar surroundings and that my role had changed. The trip changed her rejection of me to total dependency. However, there were no attempts to communicate.

The hotel room had two double beds, but Ladybug insisted on sleeping with me. We did everything together, even trips to the bathroom. When she fell asleep, she would wake up disoriented. I had to keep reassuring her that I was there and that everything was all right. By that time, I was again questioning my decision to make the trip alone with her. I was afraid to sleep, because she clung to me so tightly. We both finally fell asleep due to exhaustion. I didn't know whether to turn back or go ahead with the trip.

I let Ladybug sleep late the next morning while I got dressed. I prayed that the Lord would give her peace and take away the dreadful fear. I also prayed that God would continue to give us traveling grace for the rest of our travels. When I got her up to get dressed, she was calmer. She was quiet as I checked us out of the hotel and loaded the car to continue on our journey.

After driving for a couple of hours, we stopped for breakfast. I let her take the lead and after breakfast she wanted to walk around and look at the beautiful Georgia country side surrounding the restaurant. She loved flowers, so that put her in a better mood. The second day of traveling went well, and I relaxed a little. I avoided the mistakes I had made the day before. However, she still asked, *"Are you tired?"* or *"Are you sleepy?"* every few miles. Apparently she was afraid that I would get tired or sleepy and have an accident.

Disturbing Reunion

We arrived at my uncle's home in Gainesville, Florida early in the evening. We were both tired and weary from our travels, but at least I was happy to see my aunt. Ladybug either did not recognize her sister-in-law or was angry with her for some unknown reason. I had notified my aunt in advance that we were coming to spend a few days with her and to visit with my uncle in the hospital. However, my obvious mistake was not preparing her for my mother's condition. I wasn't sure what to tell her, because I didn't know how Ladybug would respond to her. Well the answer was not very good. For some reason, Ladybug's memories of my aunt were not happy ones and needless to say, she was very vocal if unclear about them.

In the past Ladybug had been closer to her youngest brother's wife than any of her sister-in-laws. She had traveled back and forth with her when they were having their retirement home built in Florida and visited often after they made the move to Florida permanently. So both my aunt and I were surprised at her mood. My mother's response to her favorite sister-in-law was the exact opposite of what I had hoped for.

My mother's reaction to my aunt made us all uncomfortable. I was thankful that my aunt had not gone out of her way to make a welcome dinner for us. She felt guilty because it is a Southern custom to feed guests. I urged her not to feel guilty because we had stopped for dinner earlier and were not hungry. We made it through the night without any more outbursts from my mother. Sleeping arrangements were as usual; we slept in the same bed and did everything together.

The next morning we had a silent breakfast before going to the hospital to visit with my uncle.

Ladybug did not seem to be happy or unhappy at seeing her brother. He tried joking with her as he usually did when they saw each other, but she had very little to say. She never tried to initiate conversation with him, and only answered questions he asked. Her brother was confined to bed in the hospital and that position was not familiar. When on his feet he was a jovial man of six feet, six inches tall and weighed over three hundred pounds. It is a possibility that she did not recognize this man in the hospital bed.

The first day we spent the entire day at the hospital for no other reason than I don't think my aunt knew what to do with us. She was not prepared to deal with my mother's hostility. Ladybug got restless sitting, so we walked around the hospital to stretch our legs. I took her to get something to eat and to the gift shop to buy a gift for my uncle. Shopping for the gift pleased her more than anything we had done since our arrival in Florida.

However, that evening with my aunt was even more difficult. Ladybug seemed angry with her about something that had happened in the past. In her outbursts, she would accuse her of doing and saying things that were unclear. I had to find time to explain Ladybug's illness to my aunt because she was getting upset. It made her feel a little better when I told her that my mother's memory was sometimes the direct opposite of what had really taken place and that there was no need for her to keep apologizing. So far, the vacation had not been the happy occasion I had envisioned. The unfamiliar surroundings were even more confusing for Ladybug and she was very angry.

The next day I persuaded my aunt to let me take her out to breakfast before we went to the hospital. I felt so guilty because of the way my mother was acting. Ladybug brightened up when we went to the restaurant. We didn't stay at the hospital as long that day, because my uncle wanted my aunt to take us out to dinner and to a special market to introduce me to real Southern food. We also had time to see more of Gainesville. I had not realized that it was a college town and that it had a swamp smell and appearance in some areas. However, that evening back at the house was no different. Before bed I prayed for guidance to get through the rest of the visit without any more outbursts from my mother. I had persuaded her to retire for the night early to keep from upsetting my aunt.

Surprise from the Past

The next day the Lord placed it on my heart to take Ladybug to visit a sister-in-law on my father's side of the family that lived in Sarasota Florida. The time away would give my aunt time to regain her composure without having to deal with my mother. After all she had a sick husband and needed to be there for him. I made some telephone calls to find the other aunt's telephone number, and I called to see if she wanted company. She was excited at the prospect of seeing us after so many years even after I explained about Ladybug's condition.

We left for Sarasota early in the morning while it was cool and the drive was pleasant. We went past Disney World and I tried to make Ladybug remember our visit and her favorite rides. She had enjoyed it so much I thought if she remembered the experience, I would consider stopping on the way back to my uncle's in Gainesville. However, it did not seem to matter to her, she stared at the signs blankly and did not express any desire to go there, so I canceled that idea. I only stopped once for food and gas, so we arrived in Sarasota in the early afternoon.

God had softened my mother's sister-in-law's heart prior to the call. She and my mother's relationship had been turbulent in the past to put it mildly. Both she and Ladybug had been married to brothers and shared similar adult backgrounds. They had something in common, so that could have bridged the gap over the years. My father and uncle had died two years apart leaving wives with small children. I prayed as I drove along the highway that the Lord would intervene and make the visit a happy occasion for all parties involved. Once again God heard and answered my prayer.

When we arrived, I was pleasantly surprised when Ladybug's face lit up accompanied by a big smile. She seemed to recognize her sister-in-law from her past life. That was the expression I was hoping for when she saw her brother and his wife. Ladybug followed my aunt around during the day and was more peaceful than she had been in some time. At the end of the day when we should have been leaving, Ladybug was not ready to leave, so we spent the night. Surprisingly, the unplanned one day trip turned into several days. I could not have been happier. I praised the Lord for His help.

The sleeping arrangements were the same, of course, but I had gotten use to the confusion and disorientation upon awakening in unfamiliar surroundings. Ladybug clung to me during the night. The fact that she was not tired, put us back in the not sleeping situation, but it was worth it. During the day, I was able to get some rest from the constant supervision because she would stay with my aunt when we were at her home. It was an enjoyable occasion for us because we went sightseeing and visited my aunt's adult children. All I could say to the success of the trip was Hallelujah!

At first, I didn't understand the differences between the aunts. I had no explanation for why Ladybug seemed unhappy with one and happy with the other. When I had time to think about her responses, it came to me that the second aunt was from the period when my mother had the love and support of her husband, and she was part of a happy family. There was a reason why she responded to the first aunt in a different way. Although my aunt and uncle had returned to the South after retirement, they still represented the move to Detroit which held memories of grief, fear, poverty and loneliness. It was a place where she had to make adjustments in her life without the support of adults who she had loved and depended upon.

Second Time Around

On the return trip to my uncle's home, I prayed that God would help Ladybug understand that we were only staying for a short time. I kept reminding her as we rode along the highway that we were only staying one night. I wanted Ladybug to enjoy her brother, because I knew she would probably never see him again. I got confirmation when we arrived at the hospital. I could tell by her attitude towards my aunt the second time around that she understood. She did not show happiness, but at least she was not resentful. I don't have words to express how thankful I was that my mother did not seem as angry and temperamental with her brother's wife during the second shorter visit.

We left the following day after lunch. Our next destination was Ladybug's hometown in Georgia. She was quiet as usual as we rode along the highway, only getting upset at my response when she asked, *"Are you Tired?"* or *"Are you Sleepy?"* I was not sure what she would have done had I said I was tired or sleepy. Maybe she was expecting to help with the driving, and it frustrated her when I never was sleepy or tired. I tried all of the usual things, radio, singing, and telling her funny stories, but she was not interested. The drive was short and we made good time because we only stopped to eat and rest once.

Hometown Visit

The oldest daughter of Ladybug's cousin was expecting our arrival. She was one of her favorites, so I expected a jubilant reunion. She greeted her, but she did not display any of her usual happiness at being home. She answered when spoken to, but rarely started conversations and that was unusual. At least my mother was not unhappy. She seemed to be content that she was home.

Ladybug had always loved her cousin's children, and I thanked God that this had not changed. The anger and hostility she had shown towards her brother's wife was also gone, and that was a relief. We had time to visit with my cousin and wind down before bedtime. Arriving during the daylight hours could have also been a positive because the darkness always seemed to bring out a different frame of mind in Ladybug. The sleeping arrangements had to be the same to prevent the confusion, but we both got good rest.

The visit was more fun for Ladybug because the other cousins came over to visit and welcome her home. Being the center of attention always made her happy. My mother and her cousin's oldest daughter had a lot in common, so that was also a plus. My cousin brought out an outfit that Ladybug had made and given to her on a previous visit and that pleased my mother. She even modeled the outfit to show that she could still wear it. Whether or not Ladybug remembered making it, I am not sure, but she enjoyed watching the fashion show. She seemed to really enjoy that part of her vacation.

In the past, Ladybug had loved visiting old friends and relatives when she was in town, so we spent our days doing that. I was trying to make things as they once were for her. One day my father's brother even took us to the cemetery where my father was buried. I am not sure how she felt about going to the cemetery; she did not seem to be sad. None of the visits brought about the change in cognition for which I had hoped, but I settled for what I could get. I had learned to be thankful for small things. I knew that my mother would never again be as I had known her.

I could sense that Ladybug was getting restless after a few days, so I decided to cut our visit short. I had planned to make another stop before starting for home, but Ladybug's temperament negated another stop. I thought it best to bring her back home. I was disappointed that she did not seem happier about the places we visited during our travels, but I was grateful that she did not get irate and out of control while we were away. Even though she expressed anger at my uncle's wife, she did not get aggressive with her to the point she wanted to attack her. Basically, I thought the trip was ok. It was not what I was hoping it would be. But it could have been worse.

Chapter 8
The Joys and Pains of Care Giving

Care Giving on the Road

The trip home was very hard on both of us. Ladybug seemed angry most of the time, but she could not or did not care to express why. Even stopping to eat didn't change her mood. Since she would not try to share what she was feeling, I had time to think about what might be going on in her head. It was possible that she was angry because she associated the return trip with that trip many years ago shortly after my father's death. Or, maybe she was just exhausted from all of the traveling.

It never occurred to me that Ladybug did not recognize most of the people we had visited on our trip. She never called anyone by name or talked very much at all. I thought she recognized people we saw, but I could have been mistaken. Maybe they were happy to see her, and I mistook that for her being happy to see them. I can't imagine being surrounded by people and that you do not recognize. It was probably very confusing for her. So the trip produced a lot of questions in my mind for which I did not have answers.

Again, we both grew weary of traveling, and I decided to stop for the night to rest. We happened to stop at a motel that didn't have room service, but there were a lot of restaurants nearby, like next door. Ladybug was in such a mood that I decided it was too complicated to try to take her out for food, so I ordered dinner over the telephone. When I went to pick up our orders, I left her in the room for a few minutes after telling her I would be right back. It was a mistake. When I returned, she was with a woman who had found her wandering in the hallway. I knew she was looking for me, and I was sorry I had left her.

The rest of the drive home was not much fun either. Ladybug fussed and complained all the way. It was strange that she could not carry on a conversation, but I understood a lot of what she was saying when she was unhappy or angry with me. I was never so happy to get home; at least we were in familiar surroundings. I did not regret making the trip, but I would never do it again with just the two of us. She slept very little while I was driving. I think it was because she was trying to keep me company but couldn't find the words and that aggravated her more. I prayed, "Lord help me to stay calm and not excite her while I am driving." By the Grace of God, we made it home a little worn and tired, but safe.

Care Giving Shared

Things returned to the new norm when we got back home. I had to go back to work, and Ladybug was again left in the hands of caregivers during the day. I assumed the caregiver duties during the evening hours and on weekends. I often went to work with no sleep after staying up all night with my mother. I prayed constantly while driving back and forth to work on the busy highways. Only God kept me safe. I was falling asleep at traffic lights and driving with the windows down even during the winter months. I was exhausted all the time...

On weekends when church and eating out were not options, I would take Ladybug on mini trips around the city. She acted as if every outing was a new adventure even though we went to the same places week after week. In the beginning keeping her calm on those outings caused me to be stressed almost to the point of being numb. I was always afraid she would get out of control and cause someone to try and intervene and that would be disastrous. Then I asked myself, where is your faith?

I discovered that my mother loved shopping at the Farmer's Market. It brought back old memories for both of us so I took her there most weekends. I would give her $20.00 in singles and let her buy whatever she wanted. Many times she bought the same things over and over, but that was all right, anything to keep her happy. Sometime we would buy prepared foods and fruit from the market and picnic at the park. She would be content for a while with watching the water or just walking around the park. Her attention span was very short, so I had to keep her moving.

I had to change caregivers often, sometime because of Ladybug's aggressive behavior. Many times my mother became very aggressive when the caregivers tried to control her or did not understand what she was trying to tell them. She always wanted to be in charge of every situation. The confrontations occurred mainly when they tried to stop her from doing things that were harmful to her. It did not matter to her that they were trying to protect her. She usually reacted violently when challenged. Most of them did not know how to deal with the different attitudes. For example, one day before I left for work, she wanted to leave the house. I restrained her by wrapping my arms around her. She got so angry with me, she started hitting me, and I held on to her. While she was hitting and struggling with me, I was laughing. The caregiver asked me, *"Are the blows hurting you?"*

- I said, *"Yes."*
- She then asked, *"Why are you laughing?"*
- I said, *"I could cry, but would that help anything?"*
- One of my worst nightmares was that she would hit one of them, and they would hit her back. I knew that my mother would not take that lightly.

Sometimes the caregivers did not know when Ladybug was upset with them. She would wait and tell me what they did to her. She thought they were stealing her things, and most of the time I would find them where she had misplaced them. Her frequent complaint was that they were always taking her keys, because they had them in their pockets. She did not understand that they were only following instructions. I made her a set of keys of her very own to pacify her. It was not easy sifting through what she was telling me to determine if it were true or not. Most of the time, they were innocent of wrong doing. I realized it and did not take any action. Other times, there were signs of neglect or abuse. I would speak with them and replace them if I thought their actions were inappropriate.

I had to be very careful in dealing with negative reports from Ladybug because I knew the caregivers had to be creative to keep her amused. At times, the only way they could keep her calm was by letting her put on multiple pieces of clothing. When I had to go places in the evening, I would have to peel her like an onion to undress her. It was not unusual for her to have on four or five pairs of pants. They would all be fitting correctly in the waist. I understood the reason the caregivers allowed her to put on the clothes. It must have taken her hours to get the pants on and that occupied her for hours. That was time the caregiver did not have to deal with upsetting her.

Dishonest Caregivers

While most of the experiences with caregivers were positive, I had several negative experiences during the course of Ladybug's illness. During one caregiver's tenure over three hundred dollars came up missing. First, a hundred dollar bill that I kept in a basket on top of my computer credenza came up missing. I looked all over thinking I had accidentally dropped it out somehow. I didn't realize what was happening until I made out a deposit slip for $200.00 in cash and a check to be deposited in the bank and placed it all in an envelope in my purse. I left the house to take the refuge container to the front and when I returned I found the envelope containing my driver's license and check lying on the floor next to my computer. The cash was gone.

When I confronted the caregiver, she denied taking the money.

After I let her go, I remembered going to the market several times and finding I had $40.00 or $50.00 less than I thought in my wallet when I got to check out. I also found that money had been taken from a large water bottle where I saved change. The bottle was so heavy I could not lift it. When I checked, I found it was almost empty. I learned a valuable lesson about some of the people I was leaving in charge of my mother from that experience.

I found out that one caregiver hired to take care of Ladybug was actually hungry. I discovered that food was missing from my freezer and cabinets. We had lunch together every day because she never brought a lunch. She had mentioned that she had four small children. If she had asked for food to feed them, I would have shared with her. One evening when I went to cook something from the freezer, I found very little food. So, I decided to make French fried potatoes and found no cooking oil when I had just purchased a gallon. I called the agency and asked them not to send her back again. I questioned anyone's character that would take food when they were trusted to take care of a sick love one. The agency asked if I wanted to file a complaint, and I decided against it. I thought of the four small children who would suffer more.

Crafty Mind

While on *My Ladybug's Alzheimer's Journey*, I found that intellectually she was very sharp. Not that my mother was slow normally, but some of the things she came up with were amazing. Her mind was always working. Keeping ahead of her was almost impossible. When I tried to out think her, she was usually always one up on me. When she was awake, she was always scheming on her next move. Most of the time I could see her mind working by looking in her face.

A prime example was when she insisted on trying to cook. It was all the caregivers could do to keep her out of the kitchen. It became such a problem; I decided to take the knobs off the gas range before leaving for work one day. Well, Ladybug found a pair of pliers and turned the gas on anyway. A flashback from when we had a stove without knobs and we had to use pliers to turn it on. I finally had to turn the gas off from the rear of the stove and push it back against the wall to keep her from discovering what I had done. Out of desperation, to keep peace with caregivers, I finally had to tell them to let her mix up concoctions out of whatever ingredients she could find in the kitchen as long as she could not use the range and burn herself.

At the time I did not have an explanation for why Ladybug was so fascinated with the kitchen and food. One evening we went grocery shopping. The supermarket was one of the places I could take Ladybug for an outing. However, her love for sweets made it challenging. She would fill the shopping cart with sweets, and I would have to put most of them back when we got to checkout. One evening I negotiated with her to put back all sweets she had put in the basket except an apple pie. Shopping with her took time, but it was something we could do together.

When we got home, I gave Ladybug a slice of the pie with her dinner and put the rest in the refrigerator. The next day when I got home from work, I fixed her dinner and looked for the apple pie to give her for dessert. I looked and looked for the pie and could not find it. I thought the caregiver had let her waste it or had taken it home because I didn't believe my mother had eaten the rest of the pie. When I could not find it, I gave her ice cream after her dinner and forgot about the apple pie.

The mystery of the missing apple pie was solved later that evening when Ladybug went into the kitchen and took a dish out of the oven. She brought it to me and tried to get me to eat it. It looked a little strange, so I said *"No thanks."* I happened to smell it, and it was the apple pie mixed with other things. It took a moment, but I figured out that she had remade the pie for my dinner. She could not use the stove, but she was very creative.

I found unusual ingredients mixed in the apple pie. She had used bits of newspaper and other items I could not identify in her creation. It was funny, because when I told her I didn't want to eat any at that time, but offered to give her some, she was not interested in eating it either. It occurred to me that the reason we couldn't keep her out of the kitchen was she was trying to prepare meals for me to eat when I got home from work. It was much like a wife preparing dinner for her husband when he got home from work.

Another display of Ladybug's surprising mental activities was with my cousin who was the recipient of hip replacement surgery. She was the same height as my mother and about fifty pounds heavier. It was amazing that my mother remembered that her niece was not as mobile because of the surgery. She would take advantage of her whenever it pleased her. She would walk or run away from her at will. At times Ladybug was mischievous and would take advantage of my cousin by pulling her leg in different directions to hear her scream. I am thankful that my cousin did not refuse to take care of her aunt when she was needed.

One such occasion was one day when I was in an offsite divisional meeting. To my surprise, I received an emergency page from the podium. I was taken to a telephone immediately. I called and my cousin was sobbing on the telephone. Ladybug had decided to beat up on her and they had fallen to the floor during the struggle. My cousin had kept her there as long as she could in an effort to calm her. My mother just got more aggressive. She took my cousin's leg and pulled it around the sofa. While she was explaining what was going on, my mother snatched the telephone cord out of the wall to prevent her from saying more. Thankfully, I was closer to home and got there quickly on that occasion.

I rushed home to find my mother trying to tie the door shut with the telephone cord to keep my cousin and the dog locked in the den. I asked her. *"Why are you treating your niece and Frankie that way?"* I did not receive an answer, but at least that stopped her for a moment. I reminded her that she loved them and was able to take the telephone cord away from her. When I opened the door, she gave them the blank stare that we all knew so well. The mystery to be solved was what was behind that look. She looked like my mother, but she did not act like my mother. Where was my mother?

Respite Care

The cost of caregivers for Ladybug continued to create a financial hardship. A solution was sought other than putting her in a nursing home which was not a desirable option. Literature from the Alzheimer's Association contained information about their Respite Day Care Centers which was an alternative. I called for more information to see if Ladybug was eligible for the program.

They had two locations in our area, but the one closest had no openings. So an appointment was scheduled to meet with the Program Administrator of the center with the opening. The facility and program was impressive and the cost was minimal. So I made the decision to take Ladybug there each day, although, it was in the opposite direction of my job and required additional travel time. The registration went well and my mother's response to the center was favorable. She was introduced to the other clients and my spirits were uplifted because she seemed to enjoy their company. She always liked attention, and the three men in the group surrounded her. I was pleased that she seemed to be in her comfort zone.

Ladybug began attending the Alzheimer's Respite Care Center the following Monday. I was excited about the new venture even though she did not seem to remember anything about the visit. We got up early that Monday morning so she could have breakfast before we left. I prepared her lunch and packed it in her new lunch container. There was no visible reaction to any of our activities. However, when we arrived at the center, she seemed happy to see the other attendees and had no problem with me leaving her for work.

Mid morning and noon time call reports from the Respite Carter center were very encouraging, so I was relieved and was able to get my work for the day almost completed. I was relieved and went about doing my work for the day. However, by mid afternoon, things had changed drastically. I received a call from the administrator of the Respite Care Center before I could call for a progress report. Ladybug had been fine until after lunch and the rest period. Then, she wanted to leave. Every time a door opened she wanted to leave. The situation had gotten to the point where the assistant administrator had been assigned to prevent her from running out the door and getting hurt. I was asked to come for her as soon as possible.

It took forty minutes to reach the center, and when I arrived, I found my mother sitting at one end of a six foot table and the assistant administrator who was younger and heavier than Ladybug was sitting at the other end of the table. My mother was glaring angrily at the assistant. When she saw me she rushed over to me and tried to tell me what was happening. I was so depressed at the outcome of the solution to my problem. Once Ladybug was calm, I spoke with the administrator briefly before bringing her home.

The administrator decided that eight to ten hours a day was too long for Ladybug to stay at the Respite Care Center. The long day tested her short attention span and their patience. They wanted to try a maximum of two hours a day to see if she could tolerate being there that long without episodes of aggression. That was not an acceptable solution.

I worked a minimum of eight hours a day and spent another hour and a half traveling, depending on the weather conditions. There was no way two hours a day experiment could be executed. A caregiver would have to be hired to take her to the center, bring her home again and stay with her until I arrived home from work. That would increase the expenses for taking care of Ladybug, and the goal was to decrease the expense. Another solution had to be found. I was back at the beginning with hiring another caregiver to stay with Ladybug.

Several weeks later, the other Alzheimer's Respite Care Center Administrator, near our home, called to advise me of an opening. She thought Ladybug would like it better, because it was in her old neighborhood. It was worth a try, so I took my mother to the Respite Care Center. The appointment was at 1:00 o'clock and we arrived early. However, a problem developed before we reached our destination. Ladybug was suspicious, and she would not leave the car.

I called the administrator and told her that we were in the parking lot, but my mother refused to come into the center. She suggested coming out and trying to persuade her to come in and I consented. The more she tried to get my mother to come into the center; the more upset she became. We finally agreed that maybe Respite Care was just not something she wanted to do.

Chapter 9
Alzheimer's Disease Fast Forward

It was time to fasten our seatbelts. Up to this point traveling on *My Ladybug's Alzheimer's Journey* had been rough, but doable. Signs of change were in the air. The rest of the distance would be something to behold. We had experienced brief snapshots of what it could really be like, but times were coming when there would be no letup. So far, Ladybug had proven to be outside of the box as far as predicting what the next stage the progression of Alzheimer's disease would take. I gave up trying to prepare for what was next. I just prayed that the Lord would be my refuge and strength, and a very present help in trouble as the Words say in Psalms 46:1, and He was. I knew that without His help I would not make it. I was dealing with a person that looked like my mother, but she did not act like my mother, she was acting more like my naughty child.

If I were to make it beyond this point on *My Ladybug's Alzheimer's Journey*, God would have to take control of the situation. I knew that I was not prepared for what was ahead, but I knew that God was able to keep both of us. I did not have the wisdom to make the right decisions or know what to do to make sure that my mother was at least comfortable and secure for the last miles of the journey. I had faith that God would take the helm and guide us safely to the end. My constant prayer was for the Lord to take care of her. She looked like my mother, but she did not act like my mother and probably would never be herself again mentally.

I had come to the realization that for the most part it was going to be just Ladybug and me and God on the journey. The caregivers were hired to give me relief, but the responsibility was mine alone. When I accepted that, I felt a sense of calmness come over me. My brothers were on call in emergencies, but they had their families and lives to live. Although I must give credit to my younger brother because he lived closer and was usually available when I called, no matter what he was doing. But in the midnight hours when we were all alone, I knew that I could depend on God. Whether I had to call an ambulance to transport us to the hospital or just try to entertain my mother, I was comfortable with what I had to do. God was my constant help. I was encouraged by Psalms 34:4, "I sought the Lord, and he heard me, and delivered me from all my fears."

There were many signs that my mother did not know who I was. Sometime I had the feeling that maybe she thought I was my father or just a stranger. At other times, I had no idea who she thought I was. Confirming my suspicions was not something I wanted to deal with before I was confronted with that reality. The defining moment came one Friday evening while we sat in the den watching television and talking. It had been an unusually stressful week for me at work, and I had prayed for a peaceful weekend.

At first, I thought my prayer had been answered. Something funny had happened on the television, and we were both laughing. Then she turned to me and asked, *"Well who is your mother?"* I could not speak for a moment. After struggling to compose myself, I asked her, *"Are you my mother?"* She said, *"NO"*. The surprised expression on her face was my proof. She was surprised that I asked her if she were my mother. In my mind I could hear her saying, *"How absurd?"* She looked like my mother, but clearly she was not my mother. If you have never had the experience of being disowned by a parent, I hope it never happens to you. The feeling in the pit of my stomach was unexplainable. Knowing that my mother had Alzheimer did not help me one bit.

This was one of the most difficult periods of times while on *My Ladybug's Alzheimer's Journey*. It was very difficult just watching her go through the agony. I couldn't even imagine being trapped in a time when you are alone and think a stranger is holding you captive. She tried with all of her might to get away. My heart ached sometimes from watching the pain on her face. My mother was not playing, she was very serious. If I could have eased the pain, I would have. The blank expression on her face was pretty much constant now. She was lost in a world separate from the one in which I lived. She looked like my mother, but in reality she was not my mother. She did not act like my mother.

In Another World

Regrettably, Ladybug had slipped into a place where she was most familiar. She was a young mother with small children. And to make it more confusing for her, she could not find them. Out of the confusion and frustration came a rage that would not be denied. That meant she did not have to deal with the lonely existence where she no longer felt needed, because her children were now adults. She did not have to go through the struggle of trying to control her adult children. She dealt with their independence the only way she could accept by erasing it from her mind. She denied their existence as adults. In her world her children were still infants and needed and depended on her for their very existence.

Her thinking was distorted, but her desire to find her children was very strong. She was willing to destroy any obstacle that stood between her and her children. I thanked God for deadbolt locks. It would have been near impossible to keep her from searching beyond the confines of our home. However, the locks on the doors stood between her and her infant children and that was very difficult to witness.

I learned early while on *My Ladybug's Alzheimer's Journey* that I had to put away sharp instruments. Late one afternoon when I was trying to keep her in the yard, I noticed that she had concealed a potting tool as she was frantically trying to find her crying baby. Another reason I found it necessary to hide the sharp and breakable objects was to prevent her from hurting herself. Even though I took the precautions to put away utensils, she was sharp enough to hide things she could use as weapons. So, in spite of trying to protect her from herself, I did not always succeed. It was impossible to think of all of the possible hiding places.

Distracting Ladybug when she was looking for her children was a very difficult job. She could not carry on a normal conversation, but when I asked her where she was going, she would tell me she heard the baby crying. I would ask how old the baby was, and she would say, "*He or she is two.*" My mother was like a tiger or bear defending her young. Sometimes in the beginning I would take her in the car and ask her to tell me which way to go as a calming technique. We would spend hours night and day driving around the city looking for her children. She had no idea where she was going or how to get there. If I turned the wrong way, I was met with strong resistance. Sometimes it would be a blow, other times she would just a scream.

As time progressed and Ladybug became more combative, I had to always ask someone to ride with us in the car. Ladybug would try to get out of the car or grab the steering wheel or whatever she could get her hands on. When I was too exhausted to drive, I gave her a sedative the doctor had given me so I could get some rest. I did not like to dope her up, but sometime I didn't have a choice. When she came out of it, she was on the go again. Her energy was limitless.

Substitute Children

One year a co-worker brought a "My Doll" for her daughter for Christmas. When I saw it, I got the idea that dolls might work as substitutes for Ladybug's children. I was willing to try anything to ease her pain. It would have been ideal if pictures of her young children could have been found to use as models for the dolls. But unfortunately, all pictures had been packed away to keep her from destroying the people she did not know. I took a chance and ordered two of the dolls and brought them home to her anyway. To my surprise, she loved them.

During the evenings when Ladybug was restless, I would give her the dolls and she would play with them for hours. I even took one to the hospital when she was admitted with a medical problem. I had found that she would calm down if I put the doll on her chest. In the hospital they would restrain her, and she would keep working at the restraints until I gave her the doll to draw her attention away from the restraints. People would go by her room and see the doll and think it was a real baby at first glance.

I worried unnecessarily that Ladybug would reject the dolls, because she had two sons and a daughter. I was concerned that eventually she would figure out that the dolls were girls and become angry, but she never did. She loved and took care of her babies and the gender did not seem to matter to her at all. It was not an issue after a while. Like most things on *My Ladybug's Alzheimer's Journey*, she moved on to another place and time.

I prayed for help understanding the rage that consumed my mother concerning her children. The answer came to me late one night as I watched her looking out the window pining for her babies. When she first moved to Detroit, her brothers wanted to separate her children instead of helping her provide for them as a family unit. Two of the families wanted to take my older brother and me and leave Ladybug with the baby. She became so angry she wanted to fight one of my uncles who was playing with her. She was a product of a family that had been separated and broken after the death of her mother, and no one knew the emotional scars left by that act. Apparently the hurt my mother felt at being abandoned by her brothers went very deep. In fact the hurt was so deep she feared the same thing would happen to her children.

Moving On

Ladybug lost interest in the dolls and decided that the dog was a baby and started playing with him in place of the dolls. She would dress and feed him and do all the things she would normally do for a baby. I am thankful that he never bit her, but I had to make a few trips to the emergency veterinarian hospital to take care of things she had done to him when she thought he was ill. I felt sorry for the dog, but there was no way I was going to try and stop her from taking care of him. He was devoted to her and seemed to sense that she was not herself at this time. He even became her protector. If a stranger went near her, he would growl and snap at them in defense.

However, there were days when nothing worked to distract Ladybug. One day she was determined to get her children at all costs. I tried to restrain her to prevent her from hurting herself as she tried to tear down the blinds and get out of the window. I wrapped my arms around her from behind. During the struggle, we both fell on top of the coffee table. When we fell, I was on top of her and feared that I she might have been hurt. The fact that she'd had back and heart surgery made it a serious concern. The fall did not stop her for long; she was so out of control.

I tried calling her doctor, but I could not reach him. I called "911" but got no immediate response. I called my younger brother to come and occupy her while I tried to find help. When he stepped through the door, he presented an impressive picture. A man weighing two hundred and fifty pounds and standing six feet and three inches tall did not distract Ladybug. When he heard his mother swearing like a sailor, he was shocked at what he heard and asked *"Where did she learn to talk like that?"*

- I said, *"Who are you asking?"*
- His next words were *"Ma Dea, it's me, your baby."*
- She looked at him with that dreaded blank stare and asked, *"Who?"*

Needless to say, he was crushed and tears started to roll down his face. He had not had the opportunity to experience his mother in this way. Now he knew how it felt for his mother not to recognize her child. After all, he was the love child she and my father had waited almost ten years to have. Everyone loved and spoiled him but not this time.

Before we got things under control, the neighbors, and a police car and eventually an EMS ambulance was surrounding the house. We live on the corner, so it was a real circus. While my brother was trying to compose himself, Ladybug ran out the back door with a knife. I don't know where she found it or where she was so determined to go. My brother ran in the room where I was on the telephone and said, *"She has a knife."*

I shouted at him, *"You are larger than she is, take it away from her"*. He caught her in the driveway, and she fell to the concrete as he struggled with her to take away the knife. She was lying out there flat on her back and would not let anyone help her up off the driveway. Every time one of us went near her, she would scream. My sister-in-law arrived with the granddaughter that my mother had taken care of since she was six weeks old. Ladybug would not respond to her either.

Two young uniformed police officers in full gear saved the day. I was not sure why they were there, but they were very helpful in resolving the problem. One of them sat on the driveway with Ladybug and talked to her softly until she agreed to let them help her from the cold concrete. He told her she looked like his grandmother who lived in the South, and that got her attention for some reason. After a while, he and his partner were able to get her back into the house. After getting Ladybug in the house, they explained that they were called by EMS. It seems, when a "911" call is placed and the problem is Alzheimer's disease related, they send the police to check it out before the ambulance is dispatched. The officers explained that EMS could not take patients like my mother to just any hospital emergency facility unless they were hurt or needed medical attention for something other than Alzheimer's disease. When they determined the possibility of an injury due to the fall, they called for EMS. The EMS ambulance took us to the nearest hospital, so my mother could be checked for injuries.

After fighting to keep Ladybug on the stretcher in the emergency room for over six hours, I prayed that she would never have to go to any hospital again in life. I found that hospital emergency rooms are not equipped to handle patients in my mother's conditions. Settling her was always left up to me. She was fine physically, but they did nothing to help with the Alzheimer's situation. When we returned home, I called the Alzheimer's Association hotline, and the Senior Care advisors. They explained that anytime my mother had to go to an Emergency Room, I should ask for a senior care advocate for an evaluation. They also gave me other numbers I could use to find help in dealing with her problems.

On evenings when Ladybug was not moving her belongings or furniture, she would kneel at the picture window in the living room and yell, "*Help! Help!*" and that would break my heart. I knew she was hurting, but I was at a loss as how to console her. Here I was a stranger in my own home with a mother who did not recognize her daughter or her home. She would try to break out the window in order to escape what she conceived as confinement. Today there remains visible scratches on the picture window where she tried to break her way free. I found that nothing I did helped during those times. I would just sit with her and sing softly. The sound of the desperation in her voice was like a knife cutting into my heart. All I could do was pray for peace for her and strength for me. Not only did she not look like my mother or act like my mother, she didn't think she was my mother.

Sympathetic Observers

There were occasions when the outside world got pulled into *My Ladybug's Alzheimer's Journey*. One afternoon she pulled a chair up to the kitchen sink, stepped into the sink, pulled down the curtains and tried to get out the window. One of the neighbors saw her and rang the doorbell to ask if everything was all right. He said he thought she was trying to get out, and I said she was. I did not have time to explain more, because I was busy trying to keep my mother from hurting herself. However, I did explain her condition to him later when I had more time.

The others times that I remember so well were when the school children from the school across the street wanted to help my mother. She would watch the children when they got out of school, and I think that reminded her of her children. Sometime children would ring the door bell to see if they could help when they would see Ladybug in the window. It was difficult to explain to them that she was all right. I knew they did not understand what was wrong with her and why she could not come out. It is amazing how compassionate some children are. It touched my heart that they cared enough to try and do something to help her.

In her frustration sometimes Ladybug's mood would change in a flash. I had noticed at times while we were waiting to see the doctor, she enjoyed watching fish swim around in the fish tank. I got a bright idea that buying a fish tank and gold fish for her could have a calming affect when she was agitated. So one Saturday, we went shopping for all of the supplies needed to set up the fish tank. I guess the effort was tiring for my mother, but I had not noticed.

I was so busy making sure the water was the right temperature before putting the fish in the tank, that I guess I was neglecting my mother. I was talking to her as I worked setting up the fish tank to make her a part of the process, but evidently I failed to do an adequate job. I had completed the tank setup, and the only thing left to do was put in the gold fish. When Ladybug saw me with the fish, she grabbed for them. I tried to keep the plastic bag containing the fish away from her, but she managed to grab the bag and fish flew all over the room. Then it became a job keeping her from stepping on the fish as they lay on the floor. In my mind I could hear the gold fish crunching under our feet as we stepped on them. I had to call for help to rescue the dying gold fish. Apparently she could not make the connection between the fish in the tank in the doctor's office with the one I was setting up.

I am sure Ladybug was not trying to be cruel, because she was not like that. She loved all pets and would not deliberately hurt the fish or anything else. Her inability to express herself must have played a key role in her reaction to the fish and in other situations when she appeared to be cruel. If only I could have gotten inside of her head to find out what was really going on, not only with the fish tank incident, but at other times when she became angry and combative for no apparent reason. I was concerned because these episodes occurred sometime while she was in the care of other people. The one thing I could not tolerate was to have someone respond by hitting her when she was out of control.

Chapter 10
Guardian Angels and New Adventures

One evening after I had gotten home from work and the caregiver had gone home, God sent a guardian angel to help us. He always knew what I needed most and his help was always on time. The telephone rang while I was in the bathroom and Ladybug answered before I could get to the phone. Whoever was on the other end of the line was holding a conversation with her, so I thought it was a family member or friend.

When I was finally able to get the telephone from Ladybug, I found a very nice lady on the line. She could tell that my mother was confused, and she thought she was home alone. I never found out who she was trying to reach that evening. However, she had important information for me, and I was grateful. While we were talking, someone started to bang on the front door. I excused myself to answer the door and found an EMS team responding to a call for help. They had been dispatched to my address to assist someone in trouble. I assured them that all was well and there was no emergency. When I returned to the telephone, I was surprised that the nice lady knew who was at the door. She told me that she was responsible for sending the EMS team to help my mother. When I explained the situation, she gave me numbers to call for assistance. She even gave me specific information to make sure that I spoke to the people that could help me.

I don't remember the lady's name or even if she gave it to me, but she must have been a guardian angel directed by God to call my number. The next day I called one of the numbers she had given me and reached an agency that was able to give me help with caregivers. After going through the enrollment process, they sent an experienced caregiver to take care of my mother for six hours a day and five days a week at no expense to me at any time. They also assigned a case manager and a nurse to make monthly visits. The savings for me financially were awesome; I only had to cover the remaining four hours a day while I worked. I was able to keep that service until my mother passed away. I can truly say that I made it to the end of the journey by the grace of God. I can look back and see his hand writing all along the way. Help came from many unexpected sources when I needed it most.

Out of Control

Since weekends were my time to take care of Ladybug alone, I had to take her with me to the allergist some Saturdays when a caregiver could not be found.

In the beginning I could leave her in the waiting room watching the gold fish in the fish tank. She was so preoccupied with the gold fish, she would not stray; I don't think she even realized I was gone. When she lost interest in the gold fish, it became a problem leaving her in the waiting room alone because her attention was so short, another solution had to be found.

I discovered that if I took the dog with us I could leave them in the car for a little while, and she would not leave him. I waited between twenty and thirty minutes to have the injection sites checked for reactions, so I would spend the waiting period sitting in the car with them. On this particular Saturday, when we left the allergist, Ladybug insisted that I stop the car. Experience had taught me that there was usually a reason for her behavior. I thought she needed to use the rest room, so I complied and stopped at a McDonald's Restaurant to take her to the restroom. Before I could get around the car to help her out, she had opened the door and let the dog out.

The traffic was very heavy with busy Saturday morning shoppers and I was afraid the dog would run into the street. Being a dog, he was excited to be free and wanted to run and play. I was trying to keep an eye on Ladybug and catch the dog at the same time. My mother was having as much fun as the dog. I was the only one not having fun. I was getting stressed out from chasing the dog and trying to watch Ladybug. When I finally caught him, under her protest, I put him back in the car and tried to take her to the restroom. Apparently she never had to use the bathroom, but she thought the dog needed to use it. I missed that call

I made sure I put the child proof locks on before I put Ladybug and the dog in the back seat. Getting in the car was the last thing my mother wanted to do. She got very upset when I tried to put her in the car. I had to use all of my strength, but I finally got her and the dog secured in the back seat. By the time I was ready to drive off, Ladybug was hysterical. She began to scream and shouting as I drove down the street, and that was all right until she became combative.

Since she was in the back seat, she could only hit me on the head. I thought, *"This is not a good idea while I am trying to drive."* I had to think fast to keep her from causing an accident by attacking the only part of my body visible to her. I needed to provide a target that would cause less harm and that was my recently injected right arm. So I put my arm across the back of the seat so she could hit it. After all, a swollen right arm was better than getting in an accident. Well, she pounded on my arm until it was numb. I worried about getting stopped by the police because it looked as if I were trying to kidnap her. I took the quickest route home. I knew it was dangerous, but the freeway would get us home faster. The ride was a nightmare, and I prayed all the way. The Lord brought to my remembrance the scripture, Philippians 4:13, "I can do all things through Christ which strengtheneth me". I was very grateful that we arrived home safely. I was a little battered and bruised, but safe. The reason for the stop remains a mystery even today.

Embarrassing Incidents

Regrettably, Ladybug went through a phase on her Alzheimer's journey where she would undress and lie on the floor, bed or sofa, whatever was nearest. Getting her up was a challenge, so I learned to just throw a sheet over her, not understanding what she wanted. I finally figured out much later that she thought I was my father.

In her mind, she was at the time when she was a young married woman who enjoyed sex with her husband. She always said I looked like him, so in her mind I was him. What do married people do? She was looking for a normal marital relationship. She had a need that I could not fulfill and with which I was apparently too embarrassed and unprepared to recognize. My mind would not even let me try to deal with her problem. I was ashamed to talk with her doctor or the nurse about this habit she had picked up. I know now that they could have probably given her something to help. I failed her in that area. None of the caregivers had ever mentioned that she was taking off her clothes, so I assume she was only doing it with me. That supports the theory that she thought I was her husband.

When I review some of the rough spots on *My Ladybug's Alzheimer's Journey*, I realize I could have helped her more if I had been more knowledgeable about what she was going through. If I had to go through it again, I would be better equipped to deal with the different pitfalls she faced. I regret that fear and ignorance were factors that kept me from seeking professional help in some situations. Friends and relatives meant well, but sometimes their advice was not sound.

Ladybug had continuously displayed a certain behavior that no one could understand. I should have remembered, but I didn't make the connection until much later. When she was riding in a car and nearing the house, sometimes she would try to make the driver turn the opposite way. She apparently wanted to go someplace else, but no one knew where. She would become irate and try to get out of the car or start punching the person driving the car. Even when she was with me and I turned the way she wanted to go, she did not recognize the store as the place she wanted to go.

My mother had dipped snuff since she was twelve years old. It was her secret vice. She hid it well and very few people knew about it. She had found out that a neighborhood store carried the brand she liked and would send me or one of my siblings to buy it for her. When we were out she would ask us to stop at the store to buy it before going home. In a pinch, she would even go to the store and purchase it herself but only when one of us was not available to go for her. Get this; she was ashamed to buy it herself. We used to laugh about that.

After the onset of the Alzheimer's disease, Ladybug forgot about the snuff. The few times she did remember and found a box in the house, she made such a mess with it, I was happy that she had forgotten it. Where dipping snuff had been a secret vice in the past, she was no longer embarrassed about using the snuff. She would spit it everywhere, and it was a nasty habit. Since it was a secret vice, only family members and a few close friends were aware of it. Apparently she would have flashbacks when nearing the house and would want to go to the store to buy snuff. When the driver turned the wrong way she would become aggressive, because she was not able to communicate her frustration.

I always tried to make Ladybug happy, but I am not sure I would have encouraged her to continue to dip snuff even if she had remembered. I had tried to get her to break the habit because she never used it in the presence of other people. When she was hospitalized, she would not take it with her. Sometimes she would have me slip her a box, but she would use it secretly. She had not had any snuff since prior to the back surgery. This amounted to several years since she had used it. Another mystery was solved but a little late.

Flashbacks

As I pondered over some of the incidents while on *My Ladybug's Alzheimer's Journey*, I am convinced that flashbacks were the culprit for many of the episodes she went through. For example, my cousin's home is located in the area of the city near the house where Ladybug had lived prior coming to live with me. One Friday the caregiver called to say she would be absent. I needed someone to keep Ladybug for the day. My cousin had plans for the day that prevented her from coming to take care of my mother, but she agreed to keep her at her home. So, I dropped her off on my way to work.

Everything went well during the morning hours. But my cousin had errands to run in the afternoon, so she took my mother with her in her van. When they returned to the house and got out of the van, my mother kept going down the street instead of going in the house with my cousin. She could walk and run faster than my cousin and she often did. If she decided to go someplace when she was with my cousin, she would just go. It was as if she knew that my cousin could not catch her. Brave soul that she was, my cousin sent her grandchildren to catch up with Ladybug, not to try and bring her back, but just be with her until my cousin could get back in the van and catch up with them.

It was interesting that when my cousin pulled over to the curb next to Ladybug, she got in the van with no problem. Fortunately, my cousin remembered that she had lived in the area south of her home. She remembered the street but not the address or what the house looked like. In an effort to please her aunt, my cousin knocked on doors until someone recognized my mother. When she found out the house where my mother had lived, she took her there. Thankfully, the landlady still lived there. When she came to the door, my mother walked right past her and sat down as if to say home at last.

The landlady did not remember my cousin, so she had to explain who she was and the nature of her business. She explained about Ladybug's illness and that she wanted to visit her for some reason. The lady was sympathetic and entertained my mother until she was willing to leave her home. This was the same landlady that had asked my mother to move out of the home, so I am thankful that she did not hold grudges. When I heard the story, I started taking my mother by to visit her old home in the evening when she was restless. The former landlady was very nice to my mother on those visits and would give her candy and nuts in little brown bags, which she thoroughly enjoyed. The visits worked in calming her until her mind became fixated in another area.

Mysterious Visits to the Police Precinct

Ladybug found her way to the neighborhood police precinct several times during her illness. On one occasion, she locked herself out of the house dressed in a worn house dress. One of the neighbors came to help and took her to the police station, because she told him her son was a policeman. The information was incorrect; however, they were able to locate my brother. He was a parole agent but did not work in the neighborhood. He picked her up and brought her home again.

On another occasion early one morning I got out of bed for a drink of water and to my surprise, I saw Ladybug climbing over the fence in the backyard. I had no idea how she had been able to escape from the locked gate, now I knew. By the time I put on a pair of pants, she was out of sight. While I was trying to figure out where she might be headed, I received a call from the police. I am not sure how they made the connection except we were both listed in the telephone book and had the same address.

It occurred to me that we had both gone to the police station once when someone had broken into our garage and stolen the lawnmower. Perhaps one of the officers remembered the incident. That was probably what happened because I am not sure Ladybug could tell them anything other than her name at that time. Nevertheless, I was happy they were able to contact me. When I got to the police station she would have nothing to do with me. To prevent her from getting more upset, I had to call my younger brother to come and bring her home.

I couldn't figure out where Ladybug was trying to go this time. Apparently she had stopped someone on the street for assistance and when they could not understand her they took her to the nearest police station. The reason she did not want to come with me from the police station is still unclear. When I got to the station, a police woman was trying to reason with my mother, but she was getting nowhere. When she was in that frame of mind, she would usually go with anyone except me. In her mind, apparently I was the evil stepmother or a person she did not know. This was difficult for me to accept, because she had lived with me the last time for more than ten years prior to the diagnosis. I had never abused my mother or given her any reason to fear me. I was puzzled by her reactions.

Grocery Shopping

Grocery shopping with Ladybug was always an adventure. During the early stages of her illness, she would merely follow me around in the store. However, as the disease progressed, she started picking up items and putting them in the basket without me knowing it. Checkout time would create long delays. I would find all kinds of things that I did not put in the basket and could not use. Eventually I learned to watch for the unwanted items. However, removing them from the basket was another story. Sometimes I was successful, and there were other times I was not. If she were adamant about something, it became a tug of war, and I usually gave in to her demands. Other times, she would resort to tears and tantrums in the super market.

My mother had a sweet tooth, so I would have every kind of cookie, candy and whatever she saw in my basket. Controlling the amount of sweets she ate became a challenge. I tried to avoid the bakery and snack aisles when we shopped. I would let her have cookies and candy but in moderation. Then I realized that she was trying to do a familiar thing. Shopping for groceries was something she had done most of her life.

Her choices were not good, but she didn't understand that. She considered it her responsibility to shop for groceries.

It was important to get her out of the house as much as possible, so I tried the trick of taking the dog with us when I went to the market. I would leave them in the car as I tried to run in to shop for the items I needed. That worked for a while, but as with everything else, she grew tired of that ritual. One day I was in a Meijer's store and to my surprise when I got to the check out, there was a Greeter with this lady and a little white dog. Ladybug had grown tired of waiting for me to return, so she and the dog came to find me. The Greeter was trying to explain that dogs were not allowed. Ladybug was determined that no one was touching her baby. I rushed over and told the Greeter that they belonged to me, and I would take care of them. That ended our shopping for groceries together. I would find someone to sit with her or do it on my way home from work whenever possible.

Adventures at Meal Time

In the beginning, Ladybug had a good appetite, but she eventually lost the desire to eat. I continued to cook all of her favorite foods on the weekend, but she was not eating. After thinking about the food, I noticed she was not eating that much in the evenings and on the weekends when she was in my care. I finally realized that the caregivers were eating the food that I was preparing for Ladybug. In fact, I found that my mother was eating very little of the food.

When I recognized that she was probably not getting enough nourishment, I spoke with her doctor about her food intake. He left the examining room and came back with a cup of ice cream and gave it to her. She ate most of it without stopping. He told me to give her whatever she would eat. He thought it was not important to try and keep her on any kind of diet at that stage of her illness. After that, when I took her for doctor's appointments, he always had cookies or a surprise in his pocket for her. It was sad that she was always surprised when he pulled goodies out of his pocket, not remembering the last visit.

Late one summer afternoon, I fixed our dinner and set two places at the dining room table. When Ladybug sat down, she looked at the table angrily and got up and went into the kitchen and came back with another place setting. I watched because I was not sure what she was doing. When she went to look for more food, she found none. I had learned to put all extra foods away for another meal, knowing that she probably would not eat what was on her plate. That did not stop her; she took food from her plate and put it on the extra plate.

The show was on. Ladybug picked up the dog and put him in a chair at the table. She stood looking at him for a moment. I could see her questioning how to get him close enough to eat the food. She finally decided to turn the chair around and stand him up at the back of the chair. Of course he couldn't eat that way either. She was determined that he would eat his dinner. She sat down, put the dog between her legs, and started shoveling food down his throat with a spoon. My younger brother happened to stop by during the feeding process and when he saw what was happening he said, *"Poor Frankie."* I am sure the dog was as surprised as we were when he was spoon fed. I am sure he didn't think it was very funny from the look on his face.

Another summer weekend, I had prepared our dinner again, fixed our plates and sat them on the table. Ladybug looked at me questioningly. For some reason I could not get her to sit down at the table to eat her food. She went into the kitchen and came back with a dish towel. She wrapped her plate with the towel and started out the back door. I started to stop her but decided just to follow and see where she was going to prevent a confrontation. To my surprise, she had noticed that the neighbors in back of us were having a cookout. We were not invited, but she decided she would take her own plate and join them. I stopped her at the gate and managed to get her back into the house. She was not very happy with me for preventing her from joining the party and would not eat her food.

Ladybug looked disappointed, and I felt so sorry for her. She had always loved entertaining outside and I had deprived her of that. At that moment I resolved that I would plan a cookout for her and invite family and friends. My reasons for not planning similar events were purely selfish. I was afraid of how she would act. My mother had always been an outgoing person and was a great hostess. After that I stopped isolating my mother from people and tried to be as normal as possible in our home.

I planned a birthday celebration for her in the backyard one September with all the trimmings and she loved it. She was so excited I had a time trying to settle her down enough to get dressed. She had a birthday cake with her picture on it and she was impressed. She didn't eat very much, because she was too excited. She enjoyed all of the people that attended. It was not easy preparing the food and getting ready for the celebration, but everyone helped and her happiness justified the effort I put into preparing for the event.

Communication Problems

At this point on *My Ladybug's Alzheimer's Journey*, her speech had become garbled and it was difficult to understand her, but her actions spoke louder than words. It was as if her thoughts got confused before or while she was trying to express them. I had procrastinated about taking her private telephone out because she enjoyed talking on it so much. When friends who were familiar with her condition called, they would talk with her until I was able to get the phone. They humored her even though they could not understand. However, the final straw was one year when a relative that shared the same birth date as Ladybug called to wish her a happy birthday. For some reason, I did not know that she had received the call or maybe I was not home when she called. My mother did not understand that the call was to wish her a 'happy birthday.' What it triggered in her memory was the cousin's mother.

The next day, Ladybug was determined to visit the relative's mother. The fact that she could not tell me or the caregiver where she wanted to go only frustrated her. She managed to get away from the caregiver who was slightly built and shorter than my mother. Her weight and size made it difficult for her to stop my mother once she got out of the house. Once past the caregiver, she started running up the street. When she tried to cross the street, she fell in front of a large truck with two city employees. I truly believe that God intervened again.

The driver of the truck recognized the blank stare on my mother's face because of his experience with Alzheimer's disease. He stopped to help the caregiver get Ladybug into the truck, and he drove them back home. Thinking that she was safe for the moment, the caregiver ran into the house to call and let me know what was happening. Ladybug got out of the truck and started down the street in the opposite direction. The driver came to let the caregiver know that she had gotten out of the truck and was leaving.

The next voice I heard on the telephone was that of the truck driver. He told me that my mother had gone down the street and that the caregiver was following to prevent her from getting lost. He also informed me that in her haste, the caregiver had left the house open, but that he would secure the house before leaving. I thanked him and started for home. I thanked God as I drove, because it could have been someone else. They could have taken what they wanted before leaving the house. The truck driver was so concerned he stopped that evening after work to inquire about my mother.

I called the caregiver on her cell phone and told her to stay with my mother, and I would call her again when I got into the city. It took me approximately thirty minutes to get into the city from where I worked. When I reached my exit point, I called to find out where they were and discovered that my mother had walked nearly two miles. When I caught up with them, they were at a bus stop. I pulled over, stopped the car and opened the door. Ladybug got in without hesitation. The caregiver was so upset; she refused to get in the car. She told me she would walk back to the house. It was obvious Ladybug was trying to go someplace. She was wet with perspiration from her walk, but she was determined to reach her destination.

I knew that Ladybug would not be satisfied until she reached the place she was so determine to get, so I continued to drive in the direction she was headed. My youngest brother lived in the general area, so I drove to his house. That was not where she wanted to go. She kept trying to tell me where to go, so I kept driving slowly through the neighborhoods until she finally told me to stop the car. When I stopped she got out and went to the door of this one house and knocked. I followed to see where she was going. When the door was opened by a small boy, she walked past him and went straight to a back bedroom of the house as if she knew where she was going. When I saw the lady, I knew that it was a distant cousin. Her daughter was not aware of my mother's condition and had been the one that placed the 'happy birthday' call the evening before. She explained that my mother often stopped by to visit with her mother. The mystery was solved. The next day, I called the telephone company and had her private telephone line removed.

Chapter 11
Challenging Adventures

Searching for Her Children
Most of the time Ladybug waited for me to get home from work before she tried to go on excursions, and I did not have a problem with that. I knew it was because of the Sundowner's Syndrome and tried to comply with her wishes whenever possible. One fall day after dinner, at dusk dark, we were sitting in the living room watching the headlights on cars going up and down the street. That was one of Ladybug's favorite pastime activities. I had checked all the doors to make sure they were secured, and I had put the keys in my pocket. I left her to go to the bathroom. I had been in there only a few minutes when the telephone rang. It was the neighbor's son that lived directly in back of us. He told me that my mother was at their house. I said, *"That can't be true; my mother is in the living room."* He repeated, *"She is here."*

In disbelief, I hung up the telephone and ran to check the front door; it was locked. I checked the back door; it was locked. I then checked the side door, and it was locked. As I was coming back through the kitchen,

I felt a cool breeze. I looked to my left and the rear kitchen window was raised. I thought we were having a calm and peaceful evening, and Ladybug was just waiting for an opportunity to escape.

My mother had lifted the microwave from the stand that was in front of the window and put it on the counter. This was not an easy task for a woman. She climbed on top of the microwave stand and in her frustration, kicked out the screen and climbed out of the kitchen window, which is almost six feet from the concrete below. The screen was lying beneath the window, and my mother was nowhere in sight.

When I got to the neighbor's home, I discovered they could not find Ladybug, and the neighbor was chastising her adult son because he had let her leave the house. The son was a man of about six feet tall and outweighed my mother by about a hundred pounds. There was no way she could have gotten pass him. The man kept trying to tell his mother that my mother had not gone out the door. I followed them as they went throughout the house looking for Ladybug. She was discovered in the master bedroom suite sitting quietly by the neighbor's empty bed.

I remembered that when the neighbor was ill, Ladybug would often go to visit her. Apparently she would sit by her bedside and keep her company. Exactly why that came across her mind this particular evening, I am not sure. Evidently, when the neighbor's son opened the door, she remembered visiting his mother in the bedroom. It did not seem to matter to her that there was no one in the bed. She sat there quietly by the bed.

Ladybug looked up when we entered the room. As we approached her I saw that blank determined look on her face, and I knew I was in trouble. Most of the time, she would not let me near her after she had run away from home. This time was no exception. I have tried to come up with a reason for that particular behavior but cannot. My mother seemed to be at the point in time when the neighbor was ill and she wanted to visit her. I don't think her intent was to get away from me but to comfort the neighbor. In that particular scenario, I would be the person standing in the way of her accomplishing her mission.

I called my younger brother for help once again to get Ladybug back home. Not understanding and out of frustration, my six feet three inch brother tried to remove her from the neighbor's home by force. When he lifted her from the chair, she began to kick and struggle against him causing havoc. The process was destroying the neighbor's house. So, I asked him to put her down and step outside for a moment to talk. I explained that he could not take her out by force. His approach should be to ask her to go someplace with him in his truck. She would not think he was taking her away against her will and would be more likely to go peacefully. Once he had her in the truck, he could then bring her home.

Returning home was not what Ladybug had on her mind. When she realized he was bringing her back to the place from which she had run away, she resisted with all her might. He managed to get her to the steps before he had to sit her down. He tried reasoning with her to no avail. He had to pick her up again and bring her the rest of the way. He managed to get her as far as the living room before sitting her down. She sprawled out on the floor with arms and legs flaying about. She was having a real temper tantrum.

My brother sat watching Ladybug with tears in his eyes as she thrashed about on the floor crying. It was very difficult to watch. This person looked like our mother, but she was not acting like our mother. After a while he told me he had to leave to pick up his daughter from work, but was concerned about leaving his mother so upset. I assured him that I could take care of her from that point and that she would be all right. I had learned from experience how to handle the tantrums. I left her lying on the living room floor and went into the den and pretended to watch television. When she saw that she didn't have an audience, she got up and came into the den where I was and sat down.

I was depressed because this was my mother. She looked like my mother, but she didn't act like my mother. I understood that she wanted her freedom and did not understand why I was trying to take it from her. She had always been a free spirit when it came to doing what she wanted to do. The fact that she no longer made good decisions did not register with her. She did not understand that what I was doing was because I loved her and was trying to keep her safe. I felt so helpless and alone, but I could imagine how she must have been feeling. I prayed to God for that peace that he talked about in Philippians 4:7, "And the peace of God, which passeth all understanding, shall keep your hearts and minds through Christ Jesus."

Another example of Ladybug's frustration was one evening when she was in a wandering mood. She had that familiar distant stoic look on her face, so I let her go into the backyard hoping it would pacify her. I knew that she would try to get out, but I could not think of anything else to distract her at the time. I followed her around the yard and every time she tried to climb over the fence I would pull her back. Of course she became very agitated, but I was uncomfortable with taking her out of the yard for fear of her getting out of control and running away from me.

In the past I had taken Ladybug for walks in the evening as an alternative to driving her around in the neighborhood. She had managed to get away from me several times and it was difficult getting her home again. I was uncomfortable taking her outside of the fenced yard when she was so unpredictable. She finally got so frustrated she just collapsed on the grass. I tried to encourage her to get up, but she refused assistance from me. She was in good physical condition, and I knew she could get up on her own, but my concern was for her health. The grass was damp, and the last thing I needed was for her to get sick with a cold.

Our next door neighbor arrived home to see her lying out on the grass and asked if he could help. I thought about it for a minute and decided it was worth a try. He was a man and for some reason in the past she had responded to men better than women. I had nothing to lose by letting him try to get her up. So, he came into the yard and started coaxing her to get up from the ground. She curled herself around one of his legs, and it took me ten minutes to get her unwound. When he was freed, he went back into his yard and looked over the fence and asked if she could get up on her own. He had no idea how strong she was. I thanked him for trying to help and told him I would eventually get her up.

I decided to try an approach that had worked in other situations but never when she was outside. I went into the enclosed Florida room and pretended not to be paying attention to her. When she thought she was alone, she rolled over, got up on her knees and then to her feet. She looked around and saw that no one was watching, then, she came into the house. Every time I talk with the neighbor, he recalls how strong my mother was. I always tell him how much I appreciated him for caring enough to try and help.

Caught by Surprise

I thank God for friends. One Friday a dear friend, to whom I am eternally grateful, came to the rescue. The regular caregiver called in and I had no one to take care of Ladybug for the day. The friend was on active duty in the military and had Friday as an off day. She was a good choice because of her physical training and makeup. She was the same height and size as my mother and half her age. The fact that she had experience with Alzheimer's disease was also a plus. So I was relieved when she agreed to take my mother with her for the day.

However, she did not realize that she was in for a new and unique experience. She had planned a busy day for herself but she would have no problem taking Ladybug with her. I gave her money for the things I knew my mother would pick up and refuse to put down. So they went shopping and made purchases without any unusual occurrences. Looking back, the one thing I neglected to do was to explain that Ladybug's ability to communicate and understand were probably at the level of a two year old. Therefore, she would have to be very sure of responses to questions she asked Ladybug before acting on them.

My friend had to stop by her home to prepare lunch for her ailing husband. Ladybug waited patiently for her to cook and prepare to serve the meal. When she asked my mother if she wanted to eat, her response was *"No."*. Not understanding that no meant yes, she did not prepare a place for my mother at the table. When they sat down to eat Ladybug got her purse and headed for the door. The friend thought she just wanted to go home, so she stopped her and told her she would take her home.

When she got home, my mother went to the refrigerator and took out the plate of food she had been eating earlier that morning before I left for work. The friend heated Ladybug's food in the microwave and she ate until she had had enough. When she finished eating, she fell asleep in the chair where she was sitting. The picture became clearer to me but not to my unaware friend. Ladybug was hungry and could not express it clearly to her caregiver for the day.

What my friend did not realize was that she was dealing with a mind that was always busy and that Ladybug slept very little. The mistake she made was to let down her guard by lying on the sofa in the den to rest while Ladybug was napping. Before she could react, my mother was standing over her swinging a purse at her head. She managed to get up and move around to keep from being struck with the purse. When she got past Ladybug, she grabbed her cell phone and cigarettes and ran out of the house. She forgot to take the keys and yes you got it, Ladybug locked her out of the house. Ladybug was upset with the caregiver, and she was not letting go of her anger

When I received an emergency page from our church office, I had no idea why the church would be paging me. I excused myself from the meeting to return the call. The church secretary had called to tell me that Ladybug had locked her caregiver out of the house. I realized that my mother was inside, alone and I could imagine her getting into all kind of things. Frantically, I called my younger brother who had a house key. I wanted to see if he were working in the area and could take care of the situation for me until I got there. When he arrived at the house, he called me back to say that he was in the house and everything was all right. Then I inquired where the friend was, and he said, "*She is still outside on the porch*". I asked what Ladybug was doing, and he said, "S*he is watching her through the peep hole on the door."* When I got home, I apologized to the friend for Ladybug's behavior, after we stopped laughing about her experience.

At that time I had no idea why Ladybug was so angry with the caregiver. I always tried to find reasons for her behavior to try and prevent a repeat in the future. After back tracking the events of the day with my friend, I confirmed in my mind what had happened to cause my mother to react the way she did. The food was the key element. When the friend asked my mother if she wanted to eat and she answered "*No*", the answer really meant "*Yes.*" She was angry because my friend did not give her food. She was angry and had no way of expressing her anger, so she wanted to go home. When she got home, the person with whom she was angry came with her to further frustrate her.

I did not realize the level of Ladybug's anger until the same friend invited us over for dinner the next holiday. When I went to turn into her driveway, Ladybug grabbed the steering wheel of the car. I had to pass the house to prevent an accident. I drove around until she calmed down and then returned home. My friend called to say that she thought she saw my car in front of her house, but I never came in. She asked what had happened. I had to tell her that Ladybug was still angry with her and refused to come to her house. We both got a good laugh out of her reaction. I teased her about starving my mother for a long time afterwards. That's why I thank God for friends.

An Unexpected Standoff

My dependable cousin was a special blessing to me. She encountered numerous painful experiences with Ladybug, but she never gave up. On one of several occasions when the caregiver did not come, she agreed again to take Ladybug for the day. She had a long list of errands, but she could take my mother with her as she went about taking care of her business. The morning went fine, but when she called in the afternoon to say that all had gone well, it set off an unusual set of events. She said she only had a few more places to go to complete her list of errands. I was relieved that the day was going well.

So, you can imagine my surprise when she called a few minutes later reporting that Ladybug had grabbed the cell phone away from her and became very aggressive. Fearing that she might have an accident, my cousin pulled the vehicle over and stopped. She had to get out of the car to avoid being beaten by my mother. She finally called the police for help. By the time they responded, Ladybug was throwing things out of the car in her direction. The police officers were not able to calm Ladybug. She was beyond recognizing the authority of the police. She had found an aerosol can on the floor of the van and was spraying it at anyone who came near. I will always be eternally grateful for my younger brother, because he came to the rescue again. He was able to get Ladybug out of the van and into his truck. After everything was under control, the police asked my cousin why she took her out of the house when she knew how she was. She explained that the behavior was new to her.

When we reviewed the activities just prior to the aggressive behavior, I was able to come up with a reason for the eruption. Apparently Ladybug understood that my cousin was talking about her on the cell phone. The fact that the report was positive was immaterial. Whether or not Ladybug understood that my cousin was talking to me is unclear. Apparently the fact that she was talking about her on the phone is what aggravated Ladybug. Maybe some experience from her past involved being punished because someone told on her and that triggered the behavior.

Locked Out

This time it was my cousin who got locked out of the house. The conditions were similar, but the end results were different. She was bringing Ladybug home to wait for me at the end of the day. As usually, my

My Ladybug's Alzheimer's Journey

mother wanted to go some place other than home. When my cousin slowed the vehicle to turn the corner a block from our home, my mother opened the door and jumped out and started running in the opposite direction. My cousin left the van to see if she could catch her on foot and bring her back to the vehicle or walk with her the rest of the way home. She could not catch Ladybug. So, she decided to follow her to see where she was going. In her haste to get away, my mother fell and was slow getting up. The first thing that crossed my cousin's mind was to call for help. She went upon the porch of one of the houses, but no one came to the door. However, when she looked again Ladybug had gotten up and was running again. She had not injured herself after all. She actually ran around the block with ease. In the excitement, Ladybug apparently forgot where she wanted to go because she ended up running towards the house.

My cousin only had two minutes left on her cell phone and was trying to save them for an emergency. So, she decided to unlock the door and go in the house hoping that Ladybug would follow. Ladybug saw her go in and ran pass the house. That did not work, so my cousin tried coming outside and left the door open to see if Ladybug would go inside. It never occurred to her that Ladybug would go in the house and lock her out. Yes, you guessed it. That is exactly what happened. Ladybug was a sharp thinker. She ran into the house and locked the door leaving my cousin outside. My cousin used her last two minutes to call her daughter to contact me just in case I was not at my desk. Fortunately, my brother was in the area again. When I called, he came to open the door for the caregiver.

Church Service Disruptions

While on *My Ladybug's Alzheimer's Journey*, attending church was one of the things she enjoyed most during the early part of her illness. She had always enjoyed her duties as a church usher and was faithful in witnessing and encouraging new members to join her auxiliary. There was a noticeable decrease in her involvement with the auxiliary as her illness progressed. In the beginning her friends would ask her to sit with them even when she was not able to participate in serving. I was comfortable leaving her with them and complied because it also gave me a break from the constant supervision of her activities.

However, Ladybug started misplacing her Bible as she moved from place to place in the church. That was disruptive for the other members of her auxiliary. One of them would have to come and get me to look for her Bible. She would not think about it until she saw other people with their Bibles. Then she would try to take the Bible thinking it was hers. One Sunday evening I unwisely left her Bible in the car. I had shown her that we were leaving her Bible in the car. I should have realized that she would not remember. When Ladybug saw someone with a Bible, it became a problem. I had to go out to the car in the middle of the worship service and get her Bible to pacify her. Eventually, I had to take her to sit with me where I could keep up with her Bible and try to keep her under control. I was not always successful and would have to literally pull her away from people when she wanted to take their Bibles. The problem expanded to other items. One wintry Sunday I had to forcefully drag Ladybug away from the church when she became aggressive towards a lady. She thought the lady had taken her leather gloves.

Eventually, attending church worship services became more and more of a challenge. I remember one particular Sunday when Ladybug was sitting with me. She evidently had a flashback to when I was a little girl. She stood up in church, snatched my purse from my lap and told me to get up. Everyone sitting around us was watching. I obeyed to keep from making more of a scene. I obediently followed her out to the vestibule. As we passed one of the members, she said smartly, *"We know who the mother is"*. I just smiled. When we got outside the sanctuary, she refused to give back my purse. One of the ushers saw what was happening and followed us out of the church. When she asked my mother to give the purse to her, she complied. The usher was surprised, but I did not find it unusual. For whatever reason, many times other people could get her to do things that I could not.

One event that made a major impact on my decision to limit our church attendance happened one Sunday morning. I lost complete control of a situation during the eleven o'clock worship service. I had taken my mother to the altar for prayer. The pastor knew that she was ill, and he came over to anoint her with oil and pray for her. When he started praying she fell to the floor. The pastor, associate ministers, deacons and deaconess surrounded her and prayed harder. The pastor prayed, *"Lord strengthen her legs."* I thought to myself, *"There is nothing wrong with her legs; she is just enjoying the attention."* Well, they had her surrounded and I could not get near her, so I stepped back.

After the prayer had been finished, and Ladybug was not getting up, one of the deaconesses of the church took charge of my mother and the situation. She sent for a wheelchair and told me to get my car. Without making more of a scene, I obeyed and went to the parking lot and pulled my car up to the walkway and stood by with the door opened. When a young man came to the car with my mother, he proceeded to get in the front seat on his knees to pull my mother into the car. I asked him politely to let me handle it from there. I thanked him for his help with my mother. He stood by looking puzzled as I said to her, *"Ladybug get in the car"*. She stood up and got into the car. When I drove off the man was still standing in the walkway with his mouth open.

I sincerely appreciated the prayers and concerns of the pastor and officials, but I knew that this behavior was disruptive to the worship services. Several of the members even called later that Sunday afternoon to inquire about her well being. They could not believe that she was all right. I explained that she liked being the center of attention and that she was basking in the light, and nothing more.

Disrupting the worship service was only one of the factors involved in my decision to cut back on church attendance. The other factor was Ladybug herself. She had made it almost impossible for me to give her a bath and get her dressed for church. Most of the time both of us were drenched before her bath was finished. I even tried to use church attendance to entice her to take a bath. On Sunday mornings I would drive to churches in the neighborhood thinking it would make her want to go to church, but it did not seem to matter to her anymore. In fact, I am not sure she understood what the point was. All I know is that it did not persuade her to take a bath. She was on her own schedule and would not let me give her a bath until she was ready.

Chapter 12
Frightening Experiences and Complicated Decisions

The first time Ladybug had to be rushed to the hospital following the triple bypass surgery was when she fell backwards and cut her head on the corner of a stand while leaning back in a chair in the dining room. The cut required stitches but not hospitalization. The most difficult part of the Emergency Room experience was keeping Ladybug on the stretcher. She was constantly struggling to get up, but it was nothing like the hospital stay after the triple bypass surgery. For some reason, the only person that could distract her was a security guard. He was one of God's angels of mercy. He could not spend all of his time entertaining her, but he would stop by as often as he could without being asked. He had to be the answer to my prayer because otherwise, I don't know how I could have kept her entertained for such a long time.

The bleeding had stopped decreasing the need for emergency treatment. It took a while for them to get to Ladybug to stitch up her wound. I understood, because in the Emergency Room the most critical patients got first attention. When the doctor finally got to Ladybug, her guardian angel was right there. He stayed to assist with keeping my mother calm as the doctor stitched the wound with only a local anesthesia. This did not seem to affect her cognition. The stitches did not have any visible affect on my mother. When we got home she continued to function as usual.

Swallowed Sewing Needles

Another incident I will never forget is when Ladybug swallowed three sewing needles. I have never figured out where she found the sewing needles she swallowed that evening. Well, I am getting ahead of myself. Let me start at the beginning of the incident. Late one afternoon I had just gotten home from work, said good bye to the caregiver and settled Ladybug at the kitchen counter with windmill cookies and a glass of water. I was tired so, I sat down at the dining room table to unwind from my busy day at work. She coughed a couple of times, and I prayed that she was not catching a cold. It was when she started to gag that she really got my attention. I got up from the dining room table and looked at the cookies she was eating and saw nothing unusual. I looked at the glass of water and that is when I saw the needles in the bottom of the glass. I searched her and found a whole pack of sewing needles in her pocket. I looked in her mouth to see if there was blood, and saw none. However, I could not take the chance that she had not swallowed even one. I had a feeling that the situation could be serious and headed to the hospital Emergency Room.

Upon arrival at the hospital, the security guard brought a wheel chair out to the car for her, and I went to park the car. When I returned, they had already taken Ladybug to the cardiac care unit. I am not sure why or even how they knew who she was because she was not talking anymore. At least I didn't think she was, but someone had to tell them her name. How else would they have known that she had been a cardiac patient at that hospital? The registration staff gave me directions to where my mother had been taken. When I got there she was surrounded by nurses and doctors. I explained that it was not her heart, but what I thought had happened. They took it from there.

After struggling to get Ladybug situated on the stretcher, they made arrangements to have her taken for X-rays. I waited in the area, because they thought she would remain calmer without my presence. I did not object because they seemed to be handling the situation. The staff could not believe how strong she was. It took a while to get the x-rays, because she would not lie still. When the Emergency Room doctor returned, he was holding up three fingers. How she swallowed three needles without cutting her throat was a miracle. The x-rays showed three needles in her stomach. He said they had to come out because they would tear up her insides. A special team had to be called in to do the procedure and that took several hours. I tried not to call my younger brother because I knew he had to go to work the next morning. However, I got cold and needed a coat. My younger brother came with the coat and waited with me for the surgical team to arrive.

It was after midnight when they were finally ready to scope the needles out of Ladybug's stomach. We were told that they would give her a light sedative because of her reaction to anesthesia. Then they would go to work to remove the needles. We were able to spend a few minutes with Ladybug after she was prepped for the procedure. Unfortunately, waiting in the cold waiting room was not new to us. The only difference was that we were alone in the wee hours of the morning. The surgeon came out near day break to let us know that the procedure was over. They were able to remove all three needles from her stomach. He told us they were going to admit her for twenty-four hours for observation. Since she was resting peacefully, we both decided to go to work.

After work, I returned to the hospital to find Ladybug upset and uncooperative. They were trying to make her use a bed pan and she was refusing. I walked in her room just in time to see her wetting up the floor. After I cleaned the floor, I went to the nursing station to see how she was doing and was told angrily that she could go home. I got Ladybug dressed and took her home. It is amazing how impatient some people in the medical profession can be. I knew my mother was not an easy patient because of her sickness. However she was not in control of her situation and they were.

Shocking Hospital Experience

A seizure landed Ladybug in the Emergency Room of another hospital under my protest. She had the seizure early one morning when I was getting ready for work. The caregiver had just arrived to take care of her for the day and was a great help while I called 911. I had never experienced her having a seizure, and I thanked God for the caregiver's help. The EMS Unit took her to the nearest hospital. They explained that the rule was they had to take the patient to the nearest hospital in the city. Whether or not I had other options, I did not know. I preferred taking her to the hospital where her records were and where she had two major surgeries. However, there were rules that had to be followed, and I gave in because I was concerned about Ladybug's condition.

When we arrived at the ER, my mother had recovered from the seizure and seemed to be almost back to herself. I tried to contact her doctor to have her transferred to the hospital where he was on staff, but he was out of town. His associate advised me to leave her where she was because they were overloaded with flu patients at the other hospital emergency. I was not happy to hear that news but had no other choice. I was told that my mother was being admitted and they proceeded to do a thorough workup on her to find out why she had the seizure. They found no reason, other than Alzheimer's disease patients sometime are prone to seizures. During the workup they found abnormalities in her EKG. I was unsuccessful in convincing the doctor that the irregularities were probably due to the back and triple bypass surgeries she had gone through since they had seen her at that facility. They continued to put her through a battery of tests. One of the tests was a stress test where they simulated walking on the treadmill by injecting medication to speed up Ladybug's heart. My presence was requested for the procedure because they could not keep her calm enough to do it.

Consequently, Ladybug went into cardiac arrest while I was standing by her side holding her hand and singing to keep her calm. The doctor called for assistance and they worked on her in the room before rushing her to the Intensive Care unit. I was put in the doctor's lounge in ICU to wait while they worked on her. I never felt so alone. That is when I remembered the scripture found in I Peter 5:7 "Cast all your care upon him; for he careth for you". After waiting an hour or so, one of the doctors came to tell me they didn't think she would make it.

I called the family and we waited for someone to come and talk with us about Ladybug's condition. But God had already worked it out. When the doctor came to speak with the family, she was stable, and we were finally allowed to see her. It was by the grace of God that she survived that experience. By the next day she had bounced back and was her usual uncooperative self. She proved it by pulling the IV's out of her arm. The ICU doctor said physically she was doing fine and was to be moved to a room on the cardiac floor when one was available.

I waited several days for Ladybug to be moved to another floor in the hospital. There were no beds available. The ICU staff was forced to give their attention to patients in more life threatening conditions. I stayed with my mother as much as possible to try and keep her calm. I was so frustrated after a couple of days. I asked if I could take my mother home and was told yes. I realized that Ladybug was not in a life threatening situation anymore, and that there were other patients who needed more attention. However, I did not feel better at the time since she was recovering from a life threatening condition and was receiving very little attention.

What frustrated me more than anything was that I had permission to take Ladybug home, but no one assisted me with the process. She was discharged and no one made arrangements to have her transported home. I had no idea what to do and the ICU staff was not helpful. Maybe they didn't know what to do. I am sure Ladybug must have been the first patient to be discharged to go home straight from an ICU. I finally called my younger brother, and we took her home by car. I do not think I was unreasonable in my expectations. My mother could not speak for herself, and she was a patient. I did not think she was treated fairly.

After the fact, I know she should have been sent home by ambulance. I didn't know, and the ICU staff apparently didn't know either. Ladybug seemed no worse from my brother picking her up and transferring her from a wheel chair to the car and then from the car to the house. I realized that things could have gone wrong. I prayed that she would never have to go back to that particular hospital. I prayed a lot because she was not talking. She could not tell anyone how she felt or if she were in pain, afraid or confused.

When I was not with her, there was no way of knowing if she were receiving proper care. I had to make some tough decision and prayed for guidance. I relied on Proverbs 3:5-6, "Trust in the Lord with your whole heart and lean not to your own understanding. In all thy ways acknowledge him and he shall direct your path." I trusted God to help me do what was right for her.

I know that I was not brave enough to suggest taking Ladybug home on my own. The Holy Spirit directed me, and the good Lord worked it out for good.

Retirement

I made the decision to retire from work after eight years of staying up nights with Ladybug. Not only did I stay up with her, many nights I had to call an ambulance and we were rushed to hospital Emergency Rooms for one thing or another. And there were many days and nights when I drove around the city to pacify her when I was exhausted. I know that it was nobody but God who had kept me from hurt, harm and danger as I traveled to and from work all of those years. It had come to the point where I was exhausted most of the time and did not see any relief in the near future. I had prayed about the decision and received confirmation that it was time. He had promised never to leave or forsake me in Hebrews 13:5b, so I knew that we would be all right.

Ladybug required around the clock care, and I could not continue to do all of the things required to take care of her and continue to work 40 plus hour weeks. It was not an easy decision because I was not yet eligible for social security. My mother received a below poverty level monthly income. My retirement meant I would have to take care of myself and her. I trusted God and knew that if it took all of my retirement and savings for us to live, I would do that and worry about my survival after doing all I could for my mother. I have no doubt that God would take care of our needs.

I had to put my faith in action. As a child I had been taught Hebrews 11:1,"Now faith is the substance of things hoped for, the evidence of things not seen." I also knew what Hebrews 11:6a said, "But without faith it is impossible to please him". I knew that taking care of my mother was my number one priority as taught in Exodus 20:12. I realized that it did not mean that the road would be easy. I knew I would have some hard times, and there would be times I would feel all alone, but I remembered His promises. So, I stepped out on God's word and He was with me all the way.

Ladybug had suffered with arthritis in both knees and had to wear braces prior to the back surgery and bypass heart surgeries. I am not sure why, but it did not seem to bother her during the first eight years while she was on *My Ladybug's Alzheimer's Journey*. Her mobility was better than mine as she walked, ran, climbed fences, and engaged in all types of activities imaginable. It was during that eighth year after I retired from work that she began to have trouble with falling; at least the caregivers had not reported her falling prior to that time. I talked with her doctor, and he said it was common for people in her condition and age to fall a lot. It was a fall that landed my mother in the trauma unit of the same Emergency Room that I disliked for a second time.

On this occasion, I had put Ladybug and her dog, in the backyard for fresh air. I ran into the house to get something, and while I was getting it the doorbell rang. It was a lady that had been driving past the house and saw Ladybug fall in the driveway. She had been trying to run toward the gate to escape. The gate had a lock on it, but that never stopped her from trying. She bumped her head and there was blood near her eyes. So, once again, I called 911, not realizing I had other options.

This visit revealed nothing serious, so I was allowed to bring her home again. I started to teach her to use a walker for support to prevent the falls, but she did not take to it.

A Major Emergency

Exactly one week from the first fall, Ladybug fell again. This time she was in the house. I had left her with her walker standing at the back of the sofa as I opened the blinds. I had just gotten the blinds opened when I heard the crash. My mother tried to run to the front door without the walker and had fallen head first in the step down entrance way. I was terrified. I called 911 and then called my younger brother. I told him over the telephone, *"I have killed her, I have killed her."* I just knew she was dead. When the EMS Team arrived, they said she was not dead but needed to be rushed to the hospital. The attendants worked on my mother as the ambulance sped through the streets of Detroit to the nearest hospital. It was the undesirable hospital, but at this point, I was in shock and was just grateful that she was alive. Of course I didn't mean literally that I had killed her, what I meant was that I had let her fall again and the fall might have caused her death.

The fall had broken stitches in Ladybug's right eye from where she had previously had cataract surgery. Emergency surgery had to be performed to stop the hemorrhaging. I felt so guilty, because I had let her fall. I kept asking myself why I had left her and why I didn't know that she would try to run. I kept going over and over the fall in my mind. I was so shaken I began to doubt my ability to take care of her. I had retired from work so I could be with her more, and within a year this had happened. I had tried to get her to use the walker, but she never liked using the walker. She would just drag it behind her or leave it all together. We were practicing with it the morning she fell.

The most difficult part of the surgery on her eye was waiting to hear the results. We prayed and talked about *My Ladybug's Alzheimer's Journey* while we waited for the operation to be over. Friends from church came to wait with us, and that made the waiting a little easier. Finally, the doctor came to tell us that the surgery had been a success. She would have to wear a patch over the eye until it healed, but they assured us that she would not lose her sight.

Unfortunately, Ladybug never saw out of that eye again. The anesthesia seemed to have diminished the functioning of her cognition even more than before. She was very active during her stay in the ICU unit, but somewhere between the ICU unit and the floor, she stopped moving. She had been walking when she was brought to the hospital, but she was not moving her extremities at all now. I am not sure what happened to her, and no one could explain it to me. It was as if she had a stroke, but no one confirmed that she had had a stroke. She was not paralyzed, just not moving.

I stayed by her bedside ten hours a day during her stay in the hospital. I was so consumed with guilt because I had let her fall. All I could do was read the Bible and pray. I asked the Lord for healing for my mother and strength to help me endure, but I did not seem to receive answers or I was so preoccupied with my guilt I did not recognize the answers. I was so burdened. When family members came to visit Ladybug, I still sat by her bed.

One night my sister-in-law and cousin came to visit her, and they mentioned the fact that I never left the hospital even when someone came to relieve me. I was so shaken. I never thought of leaving to go home and rest when someone came to relieve me. They assured me that they would make sure that she received her medication and was settled for the night. I apologized because I was not implying that I was the only one that knew what needed to be done for her. I left the hospital in a daze.

When I got home, I asked God to forgive me for being selfish. She was still alive, and I had faith that He would take care of her. I had to realize that God was in control and he had never left me or her. I had to rely on Him to do what was best for her. When I turned her over to Him, the heavy burden lifted from my shoulders. My prayer was answered, but in my heart I questioned if I really knew what was best for her. I had tried to take care of her and had failed. I had to realize only God knew what was best for her.

Tough Decision and Horrendous Experiences

When Ladybug was ready to be released from the hospital, I was not sure if I should take her home again. After all, she had fallen twice in two weeks, and the last fall landed her in the hospital. I questioned my ability to keep her safe. I talked with my younger brother, my backbone, and we decided that maybe we should investigate the possibility of a nursing home where trained people could take care of her. We visited several nursing facilities before settling on one. Ladybug went to the nursing facility from the hospital instead of coming back home with me.

I don't know which was worse, the guilt of letting her fall or putting her in the nursing facility. I was at the nursing facility from the beginning to the end of visiting hours. That lasted three days. On the morning of the fourth day early in the morning, I received a call that Ladybug had developed a temperature and was being taken back to the hospital. I made a decision then that if she left the hospital again; I was taking her back home. I was prepared to pay for the cost of hiring someone to assist with her care.

At this point, my decision making abilities were shaken. My younger brother was at work out of the area, so I called my cousin. She met me at the hospital. When we got to the hospital, Ladybug was not there. I called the nursing facility, and they said she had not left yet. We drove to the nursing facility, only to find that the ambulance had just left with her. When we got back to the hospital Emergency Room, she was there. To my dismay, I was not permitted to see her before the scheduled time for visitors. I explained that my mother could not speak, and they would not know her medical history. This was to no avail, I had to wait. I never felt so helpless in my life. I was frantic by the time I got to see her.

When I was finally allowed to see my mother, she was just lying there small and all alone. I refused to leave her side when the visiting period was over. I talked with the doctor, and he told me they suspected that she had some type of infection. She was admitted to the hospital, and they started treatment for the infection. They had medication going to almost every part of her body. I asked God not to let her suffer. I was drained when we finally left Ladybug in the hospital that night.

When I got home and played my messages, despair set in. I found several voice mail messages from the Emergency Room doctor saying that they had my mother in the hospital in critical condition. They were trying to contact a family member. I was so upset because I was waiting right there in the waiting room all the time. I was very distraught. I am not sure why I did not file a complaint with the hospital administration the next day, but I did not.

When I returned to the hospital to see Ladybug, the attending physician confirmed that her condition was critical and that she would not make it out of the hospital this time because of all the number of problems she had. Again I prayed that God would not let her suffer. Every day I sat by her bed and read scriptures to her and prayed until visiting hours were over. I didn't know if she knew I was there or not, but I wanted to make sure I was there if she needed me.

God sent an angel of mercy in the physician's assistant that was assigned to take care of my mother. He worked with Ladybug and me patiently and explained everything that was going on with her. If he didn't know an answer to a question, he would always find out and get back to me. I can't say the same for some of the other hospital staff that worked with Ladybug. I was very dissatisfied with the care she received while in the hospital.

Once again the physician was incorrect, and God had the last word. Ladybug did survive. I am still uncomfortable with things that happened while she was in the hospital. When I was talking with one of the doctors from the trauma unit, he indicated to me that I had let her fall two weeks in a row. That was true and I could not have felt more responsible, but that had nothing to do with her treatment while in the hospital. His remarks only added to my guilt. They also tested her to see if she could swallow and she passed the test. However, they still put in a feeding tube in her abdomen. No one bothered to explain the reason for putting in the feeding tube even though I asked. Maybe they were afraid that she would choke because she was confined to bed and did not move about on her own. An explanation would have been helpful. She did leave the hospital, but she had to go to a nursing facility for three weeks to be treated for a stool infection that the doctor said the medication could not be administered at home.

I dreaded taking Ladybug back to the nursing facility and expressed my concern to the doctor. He assured me that as soon as the last treatment was administered, I could take her home. He was true to his word. Her stay in the nursing facility was not a pleasant experience. I found that the nursing facility was apparently under staffed and not equipped to give my mother the care she needed. I had to talk with the head administrator several times and finally gave up. I prayed for the day I could take Ladybug out of there.

Chapter 13
Last Mile of the Way

Lack of Compassion

Let me pause here to say, I had serious issues with the Emergency Room personnel at one particular hospital. They did not have compassion for the patient or family members. They were unable to interpret when to enforce the rules and when to make exceptions. I had several encounters with their rigid enforcement of the rules before it was over. I hope no one will have to go through what I went through with my mother. If she had been able to speak for herself, I would not have had a problem with following the rules. That was not the case.

I talked with many of the staff members at the nursing facility and the hospitals Ladybug was in over the course of her illness. I came to the conclusion that some of the health care facilities I encountered used untrained personnel or personnel who did not have compassion for patients. Do not get me wrong. There were some beautiful people that took care of my mother, but it is that 20% who left the bad experiences in my memory. I learned that it takes a special kind of person to give to the extent that every patient is a priority. It means giving more of oneself than just a day of work. Most have it, but some do not.

I had a telephone confrontation with one doctor while Ladybug was in an unnamed hospital. I told her I did not want them to resuscitate Ladybug if she stopped breathing or her heart stopped at this point in her illness, but they should let her go peacefully. The doctor questioned why I brought her to the hospital. She asked why I didn't just keep her at home. I explained that she was laboring, and I did not want her to suffer. I wanted her to be comfortable, but if it were her time, let her go peacefully. I guess that does not make sense to everybody, but most doctors understood what I meant.

Once again I received no help when it was time for Ladybug to leave the health care facility. When the doctor released her from the nursing facility the staff did not make arrangements for transportation for her. When the doctor released her, the Social Worker's only concerns were if I were dissatisfied with the care she received. I was very unhappy; however, I was not making a formal complaint against the nursing home. I conveyed that to her. She ordered the equipment I needed to take care of my mother at home, but she failed to make arrangements for transportation. I was left with no alternative but to ask my brother to help me bring her home by car.

I was anxious to get Ladybug home in an environment where she was loved and away from the negative attitudes. She was home before the hospital bed, feeding pump, food bags and food arrived. I didn't care. I just wanted her home. The owner of the medical supply store brought the feeding pump, bags and food out around eight o'clock in the evening. He had to train me how to use the equipment.

New Experiences in Care Giving

Bringing Ladybug home bed ridden was a sobering experience for me to handle. She had never been totally confined to bed at home, even though she was restricted to the house most of the time. When my mother left home she was walking, running and sometimes falling. Now she was not mobile or verbal at all. The doctor told me she was nearing the end of her Alzheimer's Journey, and I did not question his prognosis for her life, however, I knew that God was in control. It was within His will that she lived almost five more years.

It was strange, but when I brought Ladybug home from the nursing facility, she started to move her arms and legs. She would not stand, but she could move them. She even made sounds that sounded like words. It was as if she knew she was not in the hospital or nursing facility any longer. While she was there, she chose not to respond in any way.

Taking care of my bed ridden mother was not as frightening as I had anticipated. Usually, she was in a good mood and displayed it by smiling and taking an interest in things around her. She would watch television, especially cartoons and talk back to them much as a toddler. When I played music for her, she would put her hands up like she was directing the choir. And at times she would mimic sewing with her hands. I understood that because she had been a seamstress. I also made sure she always had bed buddies to play with, and sometimes she would hold them up in the air or hug them.

One day I came in through the back door from the garage to find one of the church members who visited Ladybug clapping her hands in her face trying to get her attention. She said to her, *"Get up, and go clean the bathroom."* That is how good she looked. If one didn't know that she couldn't get up and do her normal thing, you would expect her to respond by getting up. My mother was looking at the lady with this funny expression on her face like, *"What are you doing?"* I had to laugh at the whole scene.

The caregiver that was with me the duration of my mother's confinement to bed did not have the opportunity of knowing Ladybug when she was on her feet and talking as she loved to do. However, she learned to know and love her just from taking care of her. People often questioned how I knew how she was feeling and what she wanted when she could not speak. It was much like taking care of a baby. They cannot talk or walk at first, but you love and nurture them, taking care of every need. You learn when they are happy, sad, uncomfortable, tired, and sleepy or need changing. The difference was my mother didn't cry. But she would smile when she was happy and frown when she was unhappy. She communicated with facial expressions and her hands. For instance, when I combed her hair, she would shake her hand in a fast rhythm when I was hurting her. I would apologize to her and try to be gentler. She found a way to get her point across.

There were other days when Ladybug did not want to be bothered, and she would make her body stiff. On those days we did only the things that were necessary to make her comfortable and left her alone until she was in a better mood. A case in point was when I brought her home from the nursing home; in addition to her primary home care doctor, she had been assigned two specialists, an optometrist and a podiatrist. One day the optometrist was examining her eye, and she caught him in a head lock. He could not get his head from her locked arms. The caregiver was in the room with them while I answered the door. She turned her back to do something and did not realize the doctor was having a problem until she heard the soft spoken doctor asking, *"Can I please get some assistance?"* She turned around to see my mother's arms wrapped around the doctor's neck in a head lock. We had a good laugh after he left.

There were times when Ladybug made it very clear that she didn't want to be bothered with visitors. She would close her eyes as if she were sleeping when she heard their voices. It was obvious to us that she was not asleep, but of course, the visitors would not know. The minute she heard the front door close, her eyes would open. The expressions on her face sometimes showed relief and other times mischief that she had fooled them. It proved to us, who were with her daily, that she knew what she was doing and often acted out her feelings. The medical team that worked with her also knew right away when she was having a bad day and would leave her alone.

Recognition of Special Days

The family continued to celebrate holidays and birthdays on *My Ladybug's Alzheimer's Journey* because she had loved celebrations. I had forgotten that in the very beginning, but she reminded me. I never forgot it again. Family member and friends were invited to celebrate with us in the beginning even though she was confined to bed and did not speak anymore. However, we limited celebrations to family members when it was evident that having too many people disturbed her. Friends continued to stop by to wish her a happy birthday or merry Christmas and bring flowers or balloons. However, eventually celebrations were limited to family members.

I continued to decorate her room with colorful balloons and garlands on her birthday and for Christmas holidays even if no other room in the house was decorated. Family members brought gifts like stuffed animals and musical toys for her to play with at will. Sometimes she would hug them and smile and other times she would pay no attention to them. She would usually respond when we showed her the musical toys. She shocked my cousin and me when one of the caregivers brought her a dark red stuffed animal. She would not hug it or play with it on her own. It was obvious that it was not one of her favorites. She tolerated it being in bed with her, but she never touched it unless we forced it on her. It was amazing that she still had her likes and dislikes.

Show of Emotions

My mother had never expressed love by hugging or kissing us as children. There was no doubt in our minds that she loved us, but there was no display of affection. It was when she was confined to bed that it came to me that showing affection was a behavior that had never been modeled for her as a child. Her actions when we were growing up suggested that she considered showing affection a sign of weakness. Consequently, hugs, kisses or even saying I love you were expressions absent from our lives. This is one of the epiphanies that came to me while sitting by her bedside in one of the midnight hours.

As I looked back over my life, I realized that she did not know how to show affection to her children. Even though it was never spoken, Ladybug showed love to us in thousands of ways, so there was no doubt that she loved us. It was as if life had taught her this hard lesson, and she thought she should teach us not to expect anyone to love us. When I realized that she did not show love because she never felt loved as a child, I began to love, hug and mother her.

New Relationships Formed

Our relationship took on a different direction at that time. In fact, it changed to parent and child with me being the parent. I began to show her love in every possible way. I wanted to make up for the mother's love she missed growing up. I would tell her I loved her often and I tried to demonstrate love by hugging and kissing her. She sensed the new bond between us and started looking for me when I was away. She recognized my voice and responded when I walked in her room. Visitors would ask me if she knew who I was, and my response would be "*Probably not.*" "She probably thinks I am her mother, but that is alright as long as she is happy and knows that she is loved."

Things went along pretty well during the beginning months of her total confinement to bed. The nurse came twice a week, and the doctor came once a month, unless he was called for a problem. She still did not sleep at night and even though she could not speak, I was very conscious of her being awake by the sounds she made.

I would stay awake with her and read scriptures and pray with her. Sometimes we would watch television until everything went off. Then, I would play religious music for her.

There were times when we sat quietly and did or said nothing. It was those moments that were exceptionally precious. Sometimes she would utter words that sounded like attempts at conversations. I thought I could make out what she was saying, and we would carry on conversations with one another. There would be times when I would sing, and she would attempt to join me. She could not put sentences together. But she could hear, and she understood. She did not do everything the way she had in the past, but there were still glimpses of my mother there.

Sometimes I looked back and thought about all of the lost time between us. There was so much we could have shared, but we did not understand how to do it. I truly believe God gave us the opportunity to bridge the gaps that made the difference. There are so many mothers and daughters, fathers and sons, mothers and sons and fathers and daughters who never get the opportunity we did. I would not trade those moments for anything.

Emergencies

I had to take Ladybug back to the hospital Emergency Rooms to have her feeding tube replaced several times. She was fascinated with the tube in her stomach and was always trying to pull it out. She managed to pull it out at the most inopportune times. The nursing staff could not replace it home, so she had to be transported to the hospital each time to replace it. The first time she pulled her feeding tube out, I didn't know what it was. I was preparing her food bag and happened to look around at her. I saw her holding this thing with a balloon on the end up in the air. At first glance, I wondered what it was and where she had gotten it from. I finally realized it was her feeding tube. She had this amused look on her face as if to say, *"I finally got it."* I called the doctor, and he sent an ambulance to take her to the hospital so it could be replaced. That was when I learned that I could call a private ambulance company to transport her to a hospital of my choice unless she was critical, and Medicare would pay for it.

I inquired about a band or something to put around Ladybug so she could not get at the feeding tube. I was told there was nothing. They gave me constraints for her hands, but I did not want to tie her hands. She was already confined to bed. I remembered that once upon a time babies wore belly bands to prevent them from playing with their navels until they were healed. I could not understand why there was nothing that could be done for my mother. I decided to take matters into my own hands. I went to a fabric store and brought white flannel material that could be used to wrap around her body loosely to prevent her from pulling out the feeding tube, and it worked.

Again, I had to thank the Lord for leading me to a solution. I realized it was God all the way and not me. I read in the Bible that I could ask anything and He would do it for me, and ask I did. John 14:14 says, "If ye shall **ask** any thing in my name, I will do it." What was so good, He never got tired of me asking. He just kept on answering.

Congestion was a problem that caused frequent visits to hospital Emergency Rooms with Ladybug seeking relief. The first experience I had with the congestion frightened me, and I called 911 for emergency assistance. The EMS team took her to the nearest hospital. Once again I encountered the strict enforcement of rules. Because I would not leave my mother's side and return to the waiting room, I had to stand more than seven hours one evening. I was told that chairs were not allowed in the Emergency Room. One young man was sympathetic and told me to sit on the foot of my mother's bed. As soon as the person in charge saw me sitting there she came over and told me it was against the rules for anyone to sit on the patient's bed. I got up, but God gave me the strength to stand. I stood my ground, because I was not leaving her when she could not speak for herself.

The Emergency Room doctor decided to admit my mother after the long wait. But as usual, there were no beds available. However, there was one positive that came out of the decision to admit Ladybug to the hospital. She was temporarily moved to another area of the ER where she could be monitored, and they gave me a chair to sit down. By the time they had a bed available for Ladybug, she was doing so much better that they decided to discharge her, and I was able to bring her home.

I talked with her doctor about the congestion and he told me it was peculiar to patients with feeding tubes. I had to take her to the hospital Emergency Room many nights because she sounded as if each breath would be her last. She would be looking at me as if to say, "*Help me.*" I did my best to find the relief she needed. Most of the time, her vitals were normal when she was tested at the hospital. They would admit her to the hospital for a few days and send her home. During the hospitalization the only treatments she was given were scheduled breathing treatments and sometime they would suction out the obstruction.

After numerous visits to the Emergency Room, I noticed that the staff always did the same things to resolve my mother's breathing problems. I thought I could do those things for Ladybug instead of taking her to the hospital ER so often. I asked the home care physician if he thought I could be trained to perform the functions they performed at the hospital. He agreed that I could. He was very helpful and wrote prescriptions for all of the equipment I would need.

When the equipment arrived, he made arrangements for the nurse to teach me how to use each piece of equipment. He had ordered oxygen, a nebulizer for breathing treatments and a suctioning machine. I also learned to take Ladybug's vital signs to help determine if she were in a crisis situation. I had never wanted to be a nurse or even liked being around sick people, but God gave me the strength to do what I needed to do to take care of my mother.

Even with all of the equipment and me taking her vitals often, Ladybug's congestion problem persisted. However, the training helped me to evaluate her condition and know when I should call a private ambulance and have her transported to a hospital. Of course, the hospital they would take her to was their call if they deemed that immediate treatment was required.

One evening I could hear Ladybug struggling for breath when I walked in the door. I asked the caregiver how long she had been sounding like that, and her answer was "*Not long.*" I asked what she had done for her, and she said the usual breathing treatment and oxygen. I started to try and suction her, but I thought better of it because Ladybug seemed to be in so much distress. When the caregiver left I decided to call an ambulance and have her taken to the hospital because, the one thing I could not do was check her oxygen level.

When the Emergency Team arrived, they asked all the routine questions about her condition, previous history and medication before taking her to the ambulance. God works in mysterious ways. While I was getting my coat and closing up the house, one of the attendants rang the doorbell and said they were taking her to the nearest hospital with all bells and whistles. I asked what hospital, and he told me and left me standing in the door as the ambulance with Ladybug went screaming down the street. By the time I got my car out of the garage and drove to the hospital, they were already working on her. I asked at the desk where they had taken her and was told I would have to wait until a patient advocate came out to report on her condition and take me where she was located. When the patient advocate came she told me not to worry, but it would be a little longer before I could go back. So I waited in the waiting room, not knowing what to expect.

When the Patient Advocate finally came for me and took me to where Ladybug was I almost fainted. They had put her on a respirator. That was the first time and last time I saw her on life support. The nurse gave me a telephone and told me to call my family. I just knew it was the end for my mother, this time. I called both brothers to come to the hospital. My younger brother came right away; my older brother said to keep him posted. We sat and prayed for Ladybug until they moved her to the ICU Unit.

After the Nurse in ICU got her settled, my brother left for home. The Nurse gave me a blanket and made me comfortable, and I lay there most of the night and watched the monitors. Ladybug looked so pitiful, and she was frightened because she did not understand what was happening to her and why. I prayed that she would never have to go through that process again. Her eyes seemed to be crying out to me for help, and there was nothing I could do but rub her hands. Every time she coughed, bells went off and the nurse was there. He was kind and explained what every signal meant.

He convinced me to leave the hospital just before day break because they kept it so cold in ICU that I felt frozen. He gave me his number and told me to call as often as I liked. I came home, but I did not get any rest. I showered, changed and went back to the hospital. When I arrived, the same ICU Nurse was on duty, but he was getting ready to leave. He told me that my mother was doing so well that they would probably be taking her off the respirator and out of ICU the following day. I was happy, and I was sure Ladybug was happy when they took her off the respirator that day. She looked good and they moved her to a room on another floor the very next day.

I thanked God for the new hospital, because they took very good care of Ladybug. It was the first time I had no complaints about the care she was receiving. She was taken there several more times before God gave me a solution to the congestion problem. Everyone was always kind and gave her exceptional treatment. The physician who made the home visits was not on staff at the new hospital, so Ladybug was assigned a doctor there. The doctor came and talked with me extensively about my mother's condition. She told me that it would be better if I put her under the care of a Hospice team. They could make sure she received the palliative care she needed.

Hospice Care

When I took Ladybug home I talked with her home care physician, and he thought Hospice care might be a good move. He worked with a Hospice and chose it over the ones on the list the doctor had given me. He called and made all of the arrangements for them to add Ladybug as one of their Home Hospice patients.

The Hospice team assigned to take care of my mother was very good. The nurses made regular visits and responded every time I called. I will always be grateful to them. I realized I was impatient when it came to Ladybug, but they were patient with me and helped me through every situation. Although they did not have a solution to the congestion problem they were very helpful.

Answer to the Congestion Problem

After that hospital visit, I prayed for relief from the congestion problem. I know God got tired of me begging all the time, but one night about midnight, while I was sitting next to Ladybug's bed, the Lord put babies on my mind. I thought about the solution for babies when they had problems digesting cow's milk. Since I never had children, it was not obvious to me. I went to the computer to search for baby formulas and found one with a soy base. The next morning I called around to medical supply companies to see if anyone made food for the feeding tube with a soy base and found that no one had a product I could test as a solution. I could not believe no one had ever considered using soy milk instead of cow's milk for sick patients with feeding tubes.

I prayed again to the Lord, and He led me to a pharmacy to ask about soy formulas for babies. I purchased a container of formula and went home to study the ingredients and nutrients in a serving. I counted the nutrients and thought two servings would not be enough to support an adult. So, I went to a health food store and asked if they had a soy protein product that could be added to the formula to increase the nutrients enough to support an adult body. I found that they carried exactly what I needed. I went home and started mixing the formula and soy protein and putting it in Ladybug's feeding bag. I gave it to her for a week, and there was a noticeable improvement in the congestion.

I thanked God for the success and went a step further. I added baby food to the mixture and blended it together. I tried it for Ladybug's Thanksgiving meal without any complications. In fact I made turkey and rice for her Thanksgiving dinner. I could not thank God enough for the solution, because again I knew it was not me alone who came up with the formula. The distance between trips to the ER for congestion problems expanded drastically. When the Lord called my mother home, it had been over a year since she had to be taken to a hospital Emergency Room for congestion. *Praise God*!

When I explained the change in Ladybug's condition to the doctor, he asked if I had a problem if he referred families to me who were experiencing the same problem with the feeding tube. I gladly shared the information with everyone who wanted to hear. The only problem I encountered was with Medicare. The medical supplier told me that Medicare did not want to pay for the food bags unless I was using the whole prescription. However, God was in the plan. When I explained what I was doing, they worked out a way I could continue to get the food bags.

After the respirator incident, I took measures to make sure that Ladybug was never put on life support machines again. I always rode in the ambulance with her to prevent any mistakes. I understood that even though the appropriate documents are in the patient's record, emergencies do not always allow for thorough searches of records. At that point in my mother's life, all I was looking for was something to ease her distress but not a respirator. I am thankful to God that I did not have to make many more trips to emergency rooms. The doctor was able to take care of most of the complications Ladybug experienced after that at home.

God had another plan for Ladybug's last days. When she took her last breath, she was in my arms. She went as peaceful as anyone could go. I was not caught by surprise, because her body had started to shut down after almost five years of being confined to the bed. Twelve years and eleven months is a long time to struggle with any sickness. She suffered near the end but not extensively.

Chapter 14
End of Journey

Ladybug's journey was a long one, and it ended on a wintry Sunday morning about 9:00 a.m. The journey was not an easy one, and there were many dark days. There were also some sunny days and some rainy days along the way. If the choice was available, I would make the same decision to take care of her at home. I made mistakes, but I learned a lot. The knowledge I gained on the journey would make the traveling easier but not more rewarding. There were some quiet times, some difficult times, and some moments to reflect on what was happening in Ladybug's life and why. I have no medical or scientific information to add to the Alzheimer's disease books or opinions. I feel blessed to have had the opportunity to develop the spiritual bond between my mother and me as the end drew near. I know of people who were diagnosed after my mother that were gone long before her departure. I think it had something to do with her will to live, and God appointed time for her to go home.

I counted up the years since my mother's back surgery, and it had been seven years and nine months up to the hospitalization when she lost the ability to walk. I had spent seven years and six months trying to keep up with Ladybug. Looking back over the years helped me to feel better about the falls, and I was finally able to let go of the guilt I felt. They say time flies when you are having fun. I look back and wonder where the time went. A great deal of that time, Ladybug's speech was unclear, but her mind, legs and feet carried her many places. It was by the grace of God that I made it to the last mile of *My Ladybug's Alzheimer's Journey*

Some of the decisions I made might have been different had I thought Ladybug was suffering or would have received better care in someone else's hands. That is why I will say that it was not an easy journey, but it was not all bad either. There were many uneventful days that we lived with the Alzheimer's disease and some happy days that I would not exchange for anything. I got to know my mother in a very special way, and I am eternally grateful for that. But most of all, I am thankful that I was able to give my mother that mother's love she never had.

Chapter 15
The Epilogue

God gives life, and only God should take it away. I know that according to modern standards, some might think prolonging Ladybug's life was a waste. They may think there was no quality, but I think God planned for her life to end exactly the way it did. Somewhere around the midnight hour on one of the nights she lay struggling for each breath, *"I asked the Lord Why?"* I found the answer in Mother's eyes. She was asking me for help, and I did everything within my power to make her comfortable. It took many midnights, early mornings, noon days and evening ambulance rides to hospitals and staying up all night sitting by her bedside rubbing her chest, reading scriptures, praying and singing. But it was clear to me that it was my purpose in life at that particular moment in time.

My mother could not remember having a mother's love. She missed out on the hugs and kisses and the basic nurturing mothers give their children when they are in the early developmental stages of their lives. God provided all those things Ladybug missed through me. It did not matter that I was her child and not her mother.

I am not sure when our roles reversed, but they did and it was as natural as night and day. I never had children, but God led me every step of the way as I took care of Ladybug's needs.

I am grateful to God for the opportunity to have shared in my mother's life in such a very special way. Although we shared a life of ups and downs with her at the head of the family, what we had in the end proved to be a very personal relationship that we never had previously. Words cannot express the love we shared in the last hours of her life.

It was in God's will that she waited for me to hold her in my arms before taking her last breath. We had been in the hospital Emergency Room all day. I knew she was leaving, but when the doctor asked if I wanted to take her back home, I answered yes without hesitation. We had come that far together and no way was I going to let her take her last breath in a cold sterile hospital room. It was destined that her last breath be taken in her own room in the arms of her mother.

When the ambulance brought her back home, I called the hospice nurse and asked for something to make Ladybug more comfortable, and she complied. I know that God was in the plan. It was the hospice nurse that had sent Ladybug to the hospital for something to make her comfortable. That did not happen, and only God knows why.

Everything within me says that it was God's plan for Ladybug to make her transition from this life to the next exactly as it happened. I was exhausted, because I had not slept for over 48 hours and had fallen asleep on the chase lounge next to Ladybug's bed. My Ladybug waited for me to wake up and hold her, because she wanted to say goodbye.